M000218904

Back to Shore

The Meade Lake Series, Book One

Copyright © 2020 T.D. Colbert

Published: T.D. Colbert 2020

www.tdcolbert.com

Cover Design: T.D. Colbert

For everyone who deserves a second chance.

THE MEADE LAKE SERIES

BACK TO *Shore*

T.D. COLBERT

T-minus one hour until I'm officially a divorcee.

My husband's leaving me today.

Well, technically, I'm the one doing the leaving.

I've got my bags, my belongings, my everything loaded up in my Focus, and I'm leaving. I'm sitting across from him in the courthouse right now, desperately trying not to make eye contact with him. A few more hours, and this will all be over.

"Mrs. Boughman, did you hear that?" the mediator asks me, and I nod my head.

"Yes, yes I did," I say. "Continue."

I'm moving through this like a speed racer, hyped up on adrenaline from years of letting my life crash and burn. I'm not emotional; I'm just trucking through. Luke, on the other hand, is solemn, quiet, slow-moving.

"So," the mediator goes on, "Mr. Boughman has offered to pay alimony until you have another source of income." I look up at him, forgetting my promise to myself not to make eye contact. And when our eyes finally meet, I see that his are glassy. Damnit. *Never* look him in the eye.

"You can't do that, Luke," I tell him. Damn him. This was supposed to be paperwork, the final details. Quick and painless. But there he goes, adding in the pain.

"I want to make sure you're okay, Mila," he says. I swallow. Technically, I am without a job right now. Technically, once this is over today, I'll be heading home to my parents, moving back into my childhood bedroom, starting over again at the ripe age of twenty-nine. I nod my head slowly, and the rest of the appointment seems to flash by.

We stand up, our lawyers shake hands, and then Luke looks to me, his big blue eyes pleading. He really is gorgeous. He's tall and slim with sandy hair that is always trimmed perfectly. And those big, beautiful, soul-sucking blue eyes. Ugh. I look down, gather my stuff, and head for the door.

"Mila," I hear his smooth, sweet voice say once we're in the parking lot. I freeze and turn to him slowly. He's looking down, like he's gathering his thoughts. Finally, he speaks.

"I have felt a *lot* of things over these last five years with you," he says, still looking down at his feet. "But I need you to know that one thing I *never* felt was disappointment." I scoff. Yeah, right. If marriages had titles, that would be the title of ours.

But he's serious.

"Mila, you were everything. I have a feeling you will be for a while. And I'm so sorry that things didn't work out like we planned and that I couldn't give you what you needed. But despite all the regret you have concocted in your head, the only thing I will regret about our marriage is letting things get to this point."

He takes my hand, and I go numb. He brings it to his lips and presses them against it gently, his eyes closed.

And then my ex-husband drives away, without me, back to the home we made together.

And there goes my marriage, a fiery crash and burn.

I'M LYING ON MY PARENTS' couch in their massive house, flicking through the channels on my dad's pride and joy: his 70-inch flat screen. At my feet sits the empty gallon of coffee-flavored ice cream that I've destroyed. In my hand sits a half-empty bag of sour-cream-and-onion chips, and on the coffee table sits a bottle of wine that I have sucked every last drop from.

I look around.

Honestly, it's not such a bad setup here. My parents live in the same house I grew up in—the four-bedroom Victorian house that sits on a hill at the top of our neighborhood. They still live in Kelford, the tiny little Pennsylvania town I grew up in, and when I come back here, I realize how little has changed.

Dad's retired now, although you wouldn't know it by the locals who still address him as "mayor" when he walks by.

My mom is retired from teaching but still subs on occasion when she feels she has too much time on her hands.

If it wasn't totally depressing to be mooching off my parents at this age, it would be quite the sweet life.

But I need to get my shit together. Again.

I should really be job searching. I need to get back on my feet. But I just don't have the umph. I'm tired. Physically. Emotionally. In every way possible.

I roll off the couch at the next commercial break, gather my collection of snacks, and trudge my way up the giant staircase to my old room.

But as I reach the door, I freeze. Because next door to my room is *his* room. The mahogany door is closed, as it has been since the day he died. I feel that familiar pang in my chest, then my heart starts beating a hundred miles an hour. My palms start to sweat, and I push my way into my bedroom, slamming the door behind me. I back up against it, leaning my head back.

I'm amazed at the memory of my own anxiety; I'm almost impressed by the way it can just pick right back up where it left off all those years ago. I've avoided spending a lot of time at my parents' house since I moved out—for this exact reason.

Inside my room, I smile at the way nothing has changed since I moved out when Luke and I got engaged. My mom left it all exactly the same. I fall onto my bed and into the sea of white pillows and blankets. This really was the bedroom of a teenage girl's dreams.

For starters, it's *huge*. Bigger than the master in Luke's and my townhouse. It has built-in bookshelves on the side wall, a beautiful desk in the corner, and my favorite part: a bay window with a bench.

I get up from my bed and walk over to it, sitting down in it and looking out the window. My parents have a beautiful view of the rest of the neighborhood from way up here on this hill. But from my window, I have this serene view of the woods, and in the fall and winter, you can see the creek that runs through it when the

4

leaves are gone. It's so private, so quiet from my window. It was the perfect window for him to throw rocks at every now and then…and then he stopped.

I shake my head. I lie back against the pillow and close my eyes.

FOR THE NEXT WEEK, my life looks shockingly the same as the first day I got here. I'm binge-eating every ounce of junk food in the house. I'm watching countless hours of crummy reruns and making no effort whatsoever to keep up with my personal hygiene.

On the seventh night of my depress-fest, I wake to someone shaking me.

"Oh, hey, Mom," I say, rubbing my eyes and pushing myself up from the window seat.

"Hey, yourself," she says, sitting down next to me.

"What time is it?" I ask. It's got to be past midnight.

"It's eight o'clock. I have dinner for you downstairs," Mom says. I walk across the room.

"Oh, great, thanks," I say, but just as I reach the door, she kicks it shut, making it slam and shake the whole house. I stare at her, wide-eyed.

"Hang on there, kid," she says, nodding back to the window seat. I swallow and trudge back over, hesitantly taking a seat. This is never good. This is the "we need to talk" thing.

"We need to talk," she says, sitting down next to me and crossing both her arms and her legs. I shimmy back against the glass, sitting cross-legged, waiting for her to start. It doesn't matter that I'm almost thirty. A talk from my mother still gets my nerves to stand up on their end. Especially at this point in my life, when I've done *so*

5

many things wrong, made *so* many poor choices, that I'm not even sure what she's about to bring up. I swallow again and look up at her slowly.

"So," she says, "what now?"

I look at her, raising an eyebrow in confusion.

"What...what do you mean, 'what now'?" I ask.

"You're divorced," she says. *Yes, thank you.*

"You're unemployed," she happily goes on. *Yes, thanks again.* "So, what now?"

It's not that I didn't expect this conversation in the near future; it's just that I didn't expect it the week of my divorce. I didn't expect it mere *days* after my marriage died.

"I...I don't know yet, Ma, jeez," I say, reaching up to grab a piece of my hair between my fingers and twirl it.

"Well, it's time to know," she says. My mom is a little human. She's no more than 5'2" and weighs less than I do. She's always been this way. But her size has nothing to do with the power she carries in every step, every move she makes. "I'm serious, Mila. My daughter, I love you. You have been through an awful lot in your short twenty-nine years; no one can deny that. But through all your pain, you've forgotten that you still have your own life to live. You can still make it what you want."

I don't know what to say, so I just make this weird *humph* noise. She swivels around so that she's facing me dead-on.

"Ma, Luke and I, we just didn't work out, okay? We weren't happy anymore," I say, shrugging off my marriage like it was a nail polish color that I didn't like. This answer clearly does not satisfy the wrath of Carla Walton.

"Oh, Mila, that's such bullshit," she says. My eyes widen again. My mother is hard and crass, but I'm pretty sure no one has ever loved me like she has. My dad grew up an only child, my grandfather was a lawyer, and my dad went to all the good schools and got all the best jobs. My mom grew up in a house full of nine kids and worked her ass off to get her teaching degree. She might have the sweet life as the former mayor's wife now, but she hasn't forgotten what it means to fight for things. Her no-bullshit attitude was the nightmare of my teenage self for years, but as I've aged, I now realize that it's the one thing I really should have learned from her.

"I am a firm believer that happiness is created. If you haven't been able to find happiness all these years, it's because you're keeping it at bay. You're not letting it come in. Luke…he loved you so much. And I know you loved him. But that man…he could have bought you every flower, spent every night with you, done *anything* you wanted, and you would *still* never have been happy. I know why. Do you?"

I look up at her, pleading with my eyes for her not to answer her own question.

But it's too late.

"Ryder Casey," she says.

Instinctively, anytime I have heard his name over the last decade, I roll my eyes, which is exactly what I do in this moment. His name sets off this fire in me. I push myself off the window seat and begin pacing my room, crossing my arms over my chest in defense.

"Oh, Ma, please let it go," I say. She scoffs.

"Let it *go?*" she asks, and I almost cringe at the sound of her voice. I see, out of the corner of my eye, that she's standing now, too. "Oh, honey, don't lecture *me* about letting things go. Your father and I forgave Ryder ten years ago." She makes her way to me and puts her hands on either of my shoulders.

"Honey, it's been twelve *years*. It's not healthy. The worst, most bitter kind of hate is the hate that started as love." I look up at her. "You've got to let that hate go. You've got to let Ryder go. You've got to forgive him."

She walks out of my room as swiftly as she came in, and I'm left with nothing but the stench of his name hanging in the air. I walk to my bed and sink to the floor next to it. I take a few deep breaths as if the reality of my train wreck of a life is finally hitting me.

I reach over on the floor into my duffel bag and pull out the small black journal I've carried with me for over a decade. I take a deep breath, and the first tears start to flow.

I open the journal to the middle, where I know I started the first of the letters I wrote.

RYDER,

I DON'T KNOW why I'm writing you this. I know you'll never see it, but I need to get this out. Also, just so we're clear, I'll never start one of these letters with "dear." Ever.

I WISH that when you started to hate someone, it meant that you could stop loving them instantly. But apparently, that's not how it works. And I hate that. Because I want to hate you. I wish you could take his place.

. . .

I WISH IT WERE YOU.

BUT IN THE SAME BREATH, I still love you. And I fucking hate that.

Mila

YEAH, okay.

I MIGHT NEED some help letting go.

2

I wake up the next morning with pain in my back and shoulder, and I realize quickly that it's because I fell asleep on the hardwood of my bedroom floor. Damn, I can remember a time when I could practically sleep standing up as a teenager. Now, one night without my memory-foam pillow and I may as well be an invalid.

I make my way down the huge staircase, stopping on my way to look out the stained-glass window that's halfway down the flight. I love this house. Well, I *loved* this house. Now it's full of memories that have no potential for recreation.

When I get to the kitchen, my dad is sipping his coffee at the island while my mom is finishing making eggs at the stove.

"Morning, angel," he says without looking over to me. Instead, he's engrossed in what Hoda is talking about this morning.

"Morning," I say, reaching into the cabinet for a mug.

My mom makes eyes at me but doesn't say anything. I know she can tell I had a rough night after our heart-to-heart, and I also know that she won't ask about it unless she knows I want her to.

But I decide to take the first hit.

"I'm going to find him," I say, and she almost drops her omelet on the floor. That even gets my dad's attention.

He doesn't ask who I'm talking about, which is how I know that he's in on this with my mom. Growing up, she often delivered the speeches, but I always knew that he had participated on some level.

"I think that's a good idea," Mom says, trying hard not to smile. I'm confused. I don't know what she wants out of this. I don't know why it makes her happy that I'm going to find the person who made me totally lose control of who I am. Maybe on some level, she really does think it will help.

I just think she's crazy.

"Do you think he's still—" Dad starts to say.

"Yeah. He's still there," I cut him off. Unfortunately, over a decade of separation doesn't necessarily mean that you forget everything.

"You're sure?" Mom asks. "Have you...have you been in touch with him?"

I immediately give her a look.

"Of course not," I say. "I just know he'd never leave that place—even after everything." She raises her eyebrows.

"The lake?" she asks. I nod slowly, looking down at the tattooed initials on my wrist.

"The lake," I say.

Dad gets up from the island and makes his way

toward us, throwing one arm around Mom and his other hand on my shoulder.

"Well, baby, go find him, then," he says. He walks toward a cigar box that sits on top of a desk in the corner of the sunroom. He opens and closes it and comes back with a key in his hand. He places it in my palm and wraps my fingers around it. "Do what you need to do," he says.

I nod, and after taking a sip of my coffee, I make my way back up to my room to pack a few essentials in my bag, making extra certain I have my journal with me.

This feels so silly. This feels like some sort of idiotic quest that's sure to end in nothing but more devastation and depression—two things I have had plenty of in my lifetime. But I guess I'm going because I don't really know what else I should be doing with my time…or my life. I guess I'm going because there's a chance—no matter how incredibly miniscule—that my parents might be right. That forgiving Ryder Casey, after everything that's happened, after all this time, might help me figure out what the hell I'm supposed to do with the rest of my life.

3

Meade Lake is only about a forty-minute drive across the Maryland border from Kelford, yet it feels like I've been driving for days. As I pull into the little town, I'm hit with this wave of unsettling familiarity. I haven't been here since I was seventeen, but we came here so much as kids that I know the lay of the land like the back of my hand.

Ten years. That's how long my family vacationed here in Meade Lake. My parents found a beautiful log house right on the water when I was seven years old, and they couldn't walk away. They bought it, added a boat slip, and we started coming to boat in the summers and ski in the winters—until that last summer, when I was seventeen. My dad signed a contract with a local rental company and rented it out every chance he got. My family hasn't been back here since, and honestly, if the house didn't bring in such decent income from the renters, I'm sure my parents would have sold it by now. But today, I'm not going to our house—at least, not first.

I'm driving down the highway, crossing over the

bridge, Meade Lake moving beneath me.

I drive a few more miles until I see the big wooden sign, the one he'd lifted me up onto the first night he told me he loved me.

This chill runs down my spine as I hit my blinker and make the right turn onto Big Moon Drive. I know this backwoods road scarily well. I remember how many times I kissed his neck while he drove and how guilty I felt for potentially causing *any* sort of distracted driving after… after everything.

At the end of the road, I reach the court where three of the houses lay. I look to the right, and I see it: the little cabin where he had lived with his aunt. The cabin he brought me back to the first summer I met her. The same cabin he brought me back to the one summer she was away on a trip…

My heart's thudding in my chest, and I'm almost angry at myself for the physical reaction I'm allowing these memories to have on me.

I pull up and park in the street in front of the cabin, in case I need to make a quick getaway. I hear blood rushing through my ears, and I feel my own heartbeat, but that's it. Everything else feels numb. I'm about to see Ryder Casey.

I walk slowly up the front path. There's a beat-up Ford pickup truck in the driveway, and I know it's his. I raise my fist, take a breath, and knock on the door gently. I wait a painful three seconds then knock again. I scoot a bit to the right, peeking through the window on the side of the door, but I don't see anything or anyone. I knock one more time. Surprisingly, I don't feel relief. I actually think I feel a little disappointment.

"Oh, he's not home, miss," I hear someone say. I

whip around to see a strikingly handsome black man, probably around my age, carrying a few big planks of wood down the driveway. Holy shit.

"Derrick?" I ask. He nods then narrows his eyes at me, trying to figure out who I am. Then, his eyebrows shoot up as he drops the planks and runs to me, lifting me up and spinning me around before I can even react. I squeeze him back. It's good to see him. It's been...well, the same amount of time since I've seen Ryder. He's been Ryder's best friend since they were in middle school and was with us on a lot of our journeys up here in Meade Lake.

"Girl, what are you *doing* here?" he asks, finally putting me down. "Damn, it's good to see you!"

I smile up at him. He's tall—*really* tall. He's bigger and broader than I remember but still with that same boyish smile.

"I'm just...I'm going through some things right now, and, uh...I came to talk to Ryder, I guess."

Derrick stares at me and nods. He knows everything. He was there. He knows the history. And he knows not to ask any more.

"He's covering at Lou's in town; they're down a bartender today," he says.

"He works at Lou's now?" I ask. Derrick smiles and nods.

"Among other things. I'm actually headed up to the bar myself. Do you want to follow me up there?"

I think for a second then nod.

"Sure, thanks," I say and head down to my car. All the while, I'm reminding myself that I can back out at any time. I can get there and turn right back around if I want to.

Derrick also drives a pickup truck, although, his looks to be in better shape than the one parked in Ryder's driveway. He leads me back down Big Moon Drive, onto the main highway, and in toward town. Finally, we turn into a parking lot where a small building sits. A big sign reads LOU'S LAKESIDE GRILLE. I haven't been here in so long, but I can still remember how crunchy the beer-batter fries are and how juicy the burgers are. I take a breath as I pull into the spot next to Derrick. I turn to my right and expect him to be waiting for me, but to my surprise, he hops out of his truck and trots inside, leaving me in the dust.

I follow behind him, my hand on the restaurant door. This is it. I take one more breath and open the heavy door.

The room is dimly lit, but string lights light up a stage in the corner of the room. There's a huge bar in the center of everything, and servers are scurrying about, grabbing dishes and delivering food and drinks.

I see Derrick at the bar, leaning over it.

He's whispering into someone's ear.

It's Ryder Casey.

Then, all I hear is the blood rushing through my ears again. My heart feels like it's skipping beats in my chest. My hands are sweating, and I feel a little nauseated.

Derrick turns toward the door, and then, so does Ryder. His eyes find mine instantly, and I think he must be having a similar experience to the one I'm having right this moment.

I think he's a little taller than when I last saw him. His hair is longer, too, the dark-brown chocolate waves cut off a little bit above his broad shoulders. Half of me wants to stare at him a little bit longer, memorize what he looks like now, in case I don't see him for another decade.

But the other half of me—the half of me that wins—turns on her foot and high-tails it right out of Lou's. I can't see him. I can't look at him. And I *definitely* can't talk to him.

I'm fishing for my keys out of my purse when I hear my name.

"Mila?" he asks, and I freeze against my own will. The way my name leaves his lips makes me forget what I'm doing. I hear him making his way across the gravel parking lot.

"Mila?" he asks again. I take a breath, say a quick prayer, and turn, slowly as ever, to face him.

He's close, but not too close. I was right, though; he definitely grew an inch or two after...everything. My eyes meet his big green ones once again, and I feel my body lock up.

"What...what are you doing here?" he asks. I see Derrick out of the corner of my eye. He's walking slowly out of the bar, and my instinct is to be angry with him for warning Ryder, despite the fact that his loyalty is most certainly not to me. But this wasn't how I pictured it. I pictured myself a little more in control. I pictured myself owning the situation, doing all the talking. Not the other way around.

But this was a mistake. Because, like magic, Ryder Casey wins again, and little Mila is a flimsy mess.

I fumble with my keys in my shaking hand, and my eyes meet his again.

"I shouldn't have come," I whisper, turning to my

car. "This was a mistake." My instinct is to apologize to him, but I wouldn't dare.

"Mila…" he says, and I feel my insides melting. I turn back to him. "How…how long are you here for?"

I shrug.

"I don't know yet," I say, my eyes dropping to the ground.

"Well…can we talk, maybe? Before you go?" he asks. I don't look up at him, but I nod slowly.

"Do you want to come by the cabin tomorrow? I don't work until the evening," he says. I want to say yes. I want to tell him I'll be there. But I can't give in. I can't give him all the control. I need to take some back. I need this to be on *my* terms.

"Maybe," I say. Then, I get in my car and drive away.

I pull into the driveway of the lake house—*our* family lake house—but I can't bring myself to put the car in park.

The last time I was here in this house, we were throwing everything we had brought for the summer into whatever bag we could find and speeding back to Kelford, leaving everything and anything having to do with Meade Lake in our dust.

I look up at the big, beautiful wooden house, but I can't go inside.

I pull my phone out of my purse and look up places around to stay. I find a B&B way across town on the other side of the lake. I grab dinner at a McDonald's on my way, and I call it a night by eight p.m. Lame doesn't even begin to cover it.

But seeing the once-love-of-your-life-turned-worst-enemy is freakin' exhausting.

4

I wake up the next morning in a haze. My room at the bed and breakfast is small, but it faces the lake and has this cute little walkout balcony. It's on a quiet little cove, and there's almost no boat traffic. It's so serene that I almost forget the ever-stressful situation that awaits me.

I take a breath and pull out a pair of jeans from my bag. As I'm pulling my thick chestnut locks back into a long braid, I can't help but notice my naked ring finger in the mirror. I haven't worn my wedding ring in months —ever since the "D" word first came up with Luke. But for some reason, today, it feels particularly naked.

I make my way downstairs, say good morning to Mrs. Miller, the sweet old lady that owns the place, and head out.

I drive a few minutes until I reach Big Moon Drive, and then I feel that jolt in my body that's been happening a lot the last twenty-four hours. Then, I pull up to the driveway. This time, there's a blue Tahoe parked behind the pickup truck, and I figure that must be the car he drives around town. I hear a loud noise coming from the back of the house, and I make my way around. He's standing over a table, using a circular saw on a big piece of wood.

I can't help but think about my life and how much of it he's missed. How different the Mila in front of him is than the Mila he broke all that time ago. But to me, his life looks surprisingly similar. He's still in an old flannel button-up and jeans. His hair is still messy—a little messier now that it's longer—and he's still hand-some as hell. I don't understand why he couldn't have gotten fat. Just a few pounds or a beer gut, at least. But nope, nothing. Just a perfectly preserved, slightly older version of the boy I once knew. He pauses for a moment, and that's when he looks up and sees me. I glance down into my purse, making sure my journal is there. Then, I make my way down the hill toward him. He turns everything off, dusting off his shirt and jeans and clapping his hands together.

"Hey," he says, standing straighter the second he sees me. I don't say anything; I just give him the head nod. "I'm really glad you came," he says, and I feel a slight weakness in my legs. I don't let myself smile, so I just nod again.

"Why don't we head up to the patio, and I'll get us some drinks? Sound good?" he asks.

"Yeah, okay," I say, following him up the stone path he undoubtedly laid himself. This cabin used to be his Aunt Winnie's, and each time we made a trip here, he was always making some sort of improvement to it. Even as a teenager. I heard Aunt Winnie passed away a few years ago.

I didn't call him.

The stone patio is beautiful, facing out over the trees and the lake. There's a large fire pit and a few Adirondack chairs set around it. I take a seat and look out over the water as he goes inside.

Then, I remember the time I got naked with him in that lake, and I have to look away.

He's back in a moment, and I see he's changed into a fresh white t-shirt. He sets down two glasses of lemonade on either of the chairs then takes a seat next to me.

"Thank you," I say. He settles himself, takes a sip, then turns to me.

"Mila, it's...it's good to see your face," he says. I can feel him looking at me, but I can't look back. Nope. No way. "What brings you here?"

I want to dodge this question again, but I know I can't. I know how important that question is.

And I realize it's time for Mila to take back some of the control.

I reach down into my bag and pull out my holy journal.

"I'm here for...for this, I guess," I say, motioning to it in my lap.

"What's this?" he asks. I sigh.

"This," I say, flipping through the pages, "is my journal. I started keeping it right after...everything. It's full of letters that I've been writing to you for the last twelve years."

His eyes grow wide.

"To me?" he asks. I can feel him growing a little weaker, and funnily enough, I get a little stronger.

"Yes. Every milestone I've had in my life, post-Chase, I wrote to you about. And I guess, now, I just need you to know what I went through. Without him. And without you." He's staring at me. "I came here to decide if I wanted to give these to you or not. And to decide if I could forgive you."

I decide that, for today, I'll leave out the part about my life being in shambles. We will start with the notebook and see where that goes. His eyes drop to the journal.

"You came here to...to forgive me?"

I swallow.

"I don't know yet. Maybe."

He nods, still staring down at the journal. He slowly lifts his hand, reaching out toward it. But I cover it with my own and shake my head.

"Not all at once. I need to see how this goes first before I decide if I can let you read all of these."

I flip to the first letter and tear it out of the book. I look at the paper in my hands, realizing how raw it is, how much bleeding I will do from every single old wound that has never fully healed. But I guess this is where the healing starts. I fold it in half, take a breath, and hand it to him.

"Can I read it...now?" he asks. I close my eyes and nod. He does, and I watch how his eyes scan it, narrowing when he gets to certain parts.

I can tell just when he gets to the part that says, "I wish it were you."

And then his eyebrows jump a bit when he gets to the "I still love you" part.

He swallows and folds it up, nodding slowly. I feel an ounce of guilt for a second. Just because I relive it every day of my life doesn't mean I have to make him miserable, too. I don't *have* to, but I am.

"I'm sorry, Mila," he whispers, lifting his eyes from the paper to me.

I don't know what to say. Because it's not okay. I just nod and put the journal back in my bag.

"So, what are you building back here?" I ask, nodding to the wood and tools.

"Oh, Derrick and I are building a shed back here to keep some of our tools and things in," he says. I nod. So handy. I look over to him slowly.

"I heard about Aunt Winnie, a few years back," I say, and his eyes meet mine again. "I'm sorry."

"Thank you, Mila," he says. His eyes drop to his hands, and a smile forms on his lips. "She sure did love you." I know he's not saying it to make me feel guilty, but that's what it does.

"She was great," I say, a small smile on my own lips, remembering the time she caught us up here alone and didn't tell our parents. And then I remember how that was the night we almost...and then suddenly, I can't. I can't afford a trip down Memory Lane. Not right now, with him. I stand up and dig my keys out of my bag.

"I'm going to head back to my room," I say. He stands as I do, and the cool lake breeze blows his thick locks back a bit.

"Will you come back?"

I think for a moment then nod.

"I don't think I'm done yet." He gives me a weak half-smile then says goodbye.

5

The next morning, I lie in a hammock on the shore of the lake outside the B&B, swinging back and forth as I pretend to read a book. There's one couple out here, sitting on the shore, looking out over the water, but that's it. Otherwise, it's just me, the trees, and the water, all tucked into the mountains. The sky is the deepest blue possible right now, and the sun shines through all the trees, trying desperately to touch everything. Now I remember why I loved it here so much. Why I missed Meade Lake the second I left it—because of the quiet peace it brought me when nothing else could.

But then, Meade Lake became the place that took my peace away. I felt crushed, like I couldn't breathe. I had to claw my way out of the mountains and not look back.

Or, at least, I thought I did. Until I stupidly dragged myself back here two days ago. Why do I do this to myself?

I'm trying to focus on this book, this cute little

romance novel that Molly gave me before I quit my job. I want to read. I want the world around me to dissolve. I want to go numb, like I've been for years. But after seeing his face, after our eyes met...it's like I'm feeling everything at once.

I haven't had such an overwhelming sensation since...well, since the first time Luke touched me.

God, I loved Luke. I still do. I know I do.

But when everything else is pulling you down to the bottom, love isn't strong enough to keep you afloat.

Seeing Ryder again made me feel everything, familiarity, pleasure, fear, all in one swift blow to my gut.

And yet, here I go, making plans to do it all again tomorrow.

Glad I'm not a masochist or anything.

After another hour or so, I finally give up. I walk back up the shore, around the front of the little inn, hop in my car, and drive back into town.

I'm driving down Lakeside Highway when I see Lou's again. I pull into the parking lot.

My heart begins thudding in its chest again, like a warning to my brain that is so stupidly blinded by the very attributes that made me fall in love with Ryder in the first place.

My palms start to sweat on my steering wheel with the thought of walking in and seeing his face again.

That tall, broad, hard frame.

The messy chocolate locks that I used to love running my fingers through.

The eyes...God, the eyes that told me everything I needed to know about what he was seeing, feeling...how much he loved me.

I remember so much about his body, his touch, like

how his skin always felt warmer than mine. How he was constantly playing sports or working with his hands, yet, when they touched me, they were the most gentle.

How much I needed those hands, those arms wrapped around me when I lost my brother, but how they were the last hands on earth that could be there.

As I'm staring blankly ahead at the door to Lou's, contemplating my own demise, a tap on my window makes me jump. I slap my hand to my chest as I see Derrick standing outside my driver's side door. I roll down my window and swallow back my shame.

Busted.

"He's in there," he says with a shrug, almost like a friendly warning. At first, I want to deny that I was looking for him in the first place, but I think we both know that's a load of bullshit. I nod slowly.

"Look, I was just about to go up the road a bit to grab some pie at the diner. If you're hungry, but want to, ah, avoid...whatever. You're welcome to join me," he says. I smile.

"Shirley's?" I ask. He smiles and nods.

"Shirley's."

Man, I haven't had a slice of Shirley's pie in years.

I smile and nod.

"That sounds great," I say. He smiles and taps on the roof of my car.

I get out of my car and hop into his truck.

We drive a few miles down the quiet highway that gets more and more sparse with people and cars the further out of town we go.

Shirley's is the only building for about a mile either way on the highway now. It's perched right on the side of the water, small waves lapping against the docks outside as we walk in.

"Hey there, Derrick, honey," a woman says as we head in. "Who's your friend?"

"Hey, Mabel," Derrick says. "This is Mila. She's a friend of Ryder's. He's over at Lou's tonight, so I'm showing her around. She hasn't been back to Meade Lake in a while."

Mabel smiles.

"Well, that's real nice. I know you want two slices of apple pie," she says, nodding in Derrick's direction, "but I can get you a menu, honey."

"Oh, you know what," I say, "two pieces of apple pie sounds like a good dinner to me."

Mable nods and walks back toward the kitchen as Derrick and I grab a booth. The shiny red seats glitter under the bright diner lighting, and the material sticks to my legs as I slide across it.

"So," he says after a few moments of awkward silence, "he told me you went by yesterday."

I nod.

I'm bracing for him to ask me about the letter or about why I came in the first place. I'm bracing for him to ask me for the juicy details that I'm not ready to give him.

But he doesn't.

"How did it feel, seeing him again?" he asks. My eyes grow wide, and my lips part a little. I wasn't expecting that.

Mabel puts down two waters and two plates of pie in front of us. We thank her, and Derrick digs in.

"It felt...heavy," I say after a few beats of silence. He

nods, putting his fork down after another bite and sits back.

"That makes sense," he says. I give Derrick a quick once-over. He's a very handsome man, one of those people whose looks sort of stop you where you're standing. His skin is dark, but his eyes are this light shade of speckled brown.

"So you two are still as tight as ever?" I ask, slipping a forkful of pie into my own mouth. He nods.

"Closest thing to a brother I've ever had," he says. "Well, besides my real one."

He smiles, and I chuckle.

Then, my eyes drop to the table.

A brother.

I think Derrick can sense the weight of the word.

"Look, Mila," he says, leaning back against the red leather. "I'm not sure what exactly brought you back here to Meade Lake, or to Ryder. But I want you to know that whatever you're looking for, I hope you find it. I just hope that you don't…"

His voice trails off a little bit as his eyes drop. I see him swallow, then he looks back to me.

"I know what happened destroyed you," he says so matter-of-factly that it makes me twitch in my seat. "Trust me, I won't ever forget that night. But I know you know that it destroyed him, too. But please, whatever goes on while you're here, don't…don't… He's been through a lot. I know you have too; I'm not trying to take away from that. I'm just saying, he…please, just don't…"

And then I realize he's trying to tell me not to hurt his best friend.

I stare at him, mouth agape. Half of me is shocked

he has the balls to say it to me. The other half feels my heart turning to mush. In some ways, Ryder is still the same person I once knew, the same guy who made people fall for him, who loved and was loved back so fiercely.

Finally, I nod.

"I'm not here to hurt him," I finally say. Because it's true. He nods.

We finish up our pie, and then he drives me back to my car.

I drive back to my B&B, trudge up the stairs, and collapse on my bed.

He's been through a lot.

Derrick's words echo in my ears. And I need to know what it is that Ryder has been through.

6

I wake up in my tiny room at the bed and breakfast, blinking in the bright sunlight. I left the curtains open, so I'm quite literally waking up with the sun this morning. Not that I slept well anyway. I was up all night, picturing him. Thinking about him. Almost letting my guard down enough to smile at the thought of his smile. But I don't. Because I still hate him.

I think.

I stop in town at a small cafe I find, order a cup of coffee and a muffin, and sit down in a big chair at the very back of the restaurant. There's a cozy fireplace in the corner, and I can see the water out the front windows. I forgot how serene this place is, how much it can make you forget. I brush the crumbs off my lap and hop to my feet.

Day two, letter two. Let's do this.

I drive a few miles down the road till I reach Big Moon Drive, but when I pull up to the cabin, I see something taped to the front door, and the Tahoe is gone. I make my way up the few porch steps and see that the piece of paper has my name on it.

MILA,

>Had to work at the store today. Feel free to come by.
>1134 Lakeside Hwy

I HOPE YOU COME.

>Ryder

I REREAD the "I hope you come" line a few times, and it gives my stomach this little flip feeling. I take a breath, plug the address into my phone, and get back in my car. I only drive for about seven or eight minutes until I pull up to the store.

A big sign above the door reads BIG MOON WATER & SKI SHOP. It didn't occur to me which store he was talking about in the note. Does he own this? I park my car and pull my notebook out of my bag. I flip to letter number two.

RYDER,

I'M STARTING COLLEGE TODAY. Mom got me all this awesome stuff for my dorm room, my classes are all set, and I really like my roommate. But all I can think about is how my brother should be here with me. About how much easier it would be for me if he were here. And about how excited he was to go to UMD with me.

. . .

Mila

I HAVEN'T REREAD some of these older ones in years, and the pain is fresh and raw, like a scab reopening.

When I finally make my way inside the store, I realize how jam-packed it is. There are ski clothes on racks in the back of the store and bathing suits at the front. There are boogie boards and water skis on racks on the ceiling and skis and snowboards in the corners. There's a huge line of people that's wrapping around the front of the store. At the front counter, I see Derrick handing people forms and entering things into the register. Then, in some sort of majestic entrance, Ryder appears down the large wooden staircase at the corner of the shop. He's carrying a big stack of papers and has a few life vests looped around his muscular arm. He smiles at a few of the customers and hands the vests off to a group of them at the front. Then he makes his way behind the counter with Derrick and starts handing out the forms himself.

"Yep, just sign right here, and then you can head down the path across the street to the lake, and they will get you set up with a kayak. Yep, no problem," I hear him say. His smile is just as dazzling as I remember. And as I catch myself staring at those pearly whites, I realize how dangerous that thought is. I shake my head as I continue watching him and Derrick operating so seamlessly despite the snake of a line that awaits them. Finally, as the crowd dwindles down, he looks up from the counter, and our eyes meet.

A slow smile spreads across his lips, and I fight hard against my body not to let my stomach flip.

I lose the battle.

"You came," he says quietly, making his way out from behind the counter. Out of the corner of my eye, I see Derrick watching us. But I can't focus on that because Ryder Casey is making his way to me. And as he gets to me, he reaches a hand out to my arm. I stand back, but not before his fingertips brush my forearm. My eyes dart up to his, and his eyebrows shoot up. This is the first time we've actually come in physical contact with each other in over a decade. I feel my heart racing, and I know he can sense it. His eyes drop in shame.

I'm glad he realized there are still boundaries between us. But at the same time, I can't help but feel a little bit of relief in realizing how happy he was to see me.

"Hey, um, I think we're good here for a bit if you guys wanted to catch up," Derrick mutters just in the nick of awkward time.

"Oh, yeah, thanks, D," Ryder says, holding a hand out toward the door. I nod and thank Derrick as I step outside, thankful for the fresh air. I wonder if he mentioned to Ryder that we got together last night, but I decide against bringing it up.

The lake is as big and blue as I remember, filled with buzzing boats and trails in the water.

I follow Ryder around the side of the building to a path that leads through some tall pines. There's a bench a few feet ahead, and he stops when he reaches it, plopping down and taking a deep breath.

I sit down next to him, careful to leave a lot of space between us.

"I'm really glad you came by," he says. "I was worried I wasn't going to see you again."

His bluntness takes me by surprise.

"Do you own that store?" I ask him, desperate to change the subject.

"I do. Well, I co-own it, with Derrick. We opened it about two years ago," he says.

"Wow, that's great. It looks like business is good," I say. He smiles.

"It is," he says, "but there's a *lot* of work that goes into it."

I smile and lean back against the bench. The water is so blue it almost looks fake. It's choppy because of the wind and the boats, but it's still so calming to just watch it, listen to it lap against the shoreline.

"So," he finally says, clearing his throat and turning more to face me. "Do I get another letter today?" His mouth forms into this half-smile that fades just as quickly as it appears. I quickly smile back, reaching for my notebook in my bag. I take in a deep breath. I know this one is going to hurt him.

"Yeah," I say, pulling the piece of paper out of the notebook and handing it to him slowly. He takes a breath, too, like he's waiting for the blow.

I look back out at the water while he reads it, my breath shallow in my throat. When he's done, he folds it in half and puts it on his knee, patting it.

"I'm sorry, Mila," he whispers, and I feel this searing pain through my chest. He should be sorry. He should be so, so sorry. But I am the one feeling sorry right now, and I don't know exactly why.

I give him another quick, painfully fake half-smile before putting the notebook away.

"I think about that a lot," he says, looking out over the lake.

"About what?"

"College. Just what he would have done. If he would have gone on to play in the NFL. And if we would have made it long-distance," he says, still looking out over the water. My eyes flash to him.

I remember that pain so clearly—not the pain of losing my brother, but the pain of wondering whether or not I was going to lose Ryder. You know, before I *actually* lost him. Before I lost them both.

I follow his gaze out over the lake.

"I think about it a lot, too," I say.

He turns back to me.

"Can I ask you something?" he asks. I nod. "Why now? Why, after all this time, did you come back now?"

I look out over the water now, as if the answer is going to pop up on a wake or something.

"I'm…I'm going through some things. And I just felt like it was time to put this all behind me," I say. I flick my eyes to his, and he narrows his at me.

"And to put us behind you?" he asks. I swallow. In theory, "us" should have been behind me a long time ago. I look back out over the water.

"There is no 'us,' Ryder," I say.

"Aw, Mila, there's always been 'us.' And there always will be," he says, lifting his eyes to mine and staring into them so deeply that I blush. His radio buzzes on his hip, and he presses a button and tells Derrick he'll be right up.

I sit on the bench a little while longer, looking out over the water.

There's always been us. And there always will be.

Damnit.

He's probably right.

7

L ater that evening, I'm sitting on the back deck of the B&B, flipping through some pages of the book that I'm convinced I'm never going to be focused enough to read. I look out across the lake, which is turning a deep-navy color as the sun slips away behind the mountains, when my phone buzzes on the arm of my Adirondack chair.

"Hey, Mom," I say.

"How's it going?" she asks.

"Did you find him yet?" I hear my dad ask in the background. I scoff.

"Well, Dad just gets right to it, doesn't he?" I ask.

I can practically hear Mom shrug through the phone.

"No sense beating around the bush," she says. "Well, have you?"

"Yeah, I have," I say. I hear Mom let out a little gasp.

"And?"

"How did it go?" Dad asks. "Do you feel better?"

I pause for a minute, recounting the few run-ins I've had with him.

I think when I saw him again after all these years, I was expecting some sort of huge, life-altering halt, like a ton of bricks crushing me. Like I was being smothered, drowned, unable to breathe.

Except, when I first laid eyes on Ryder again after twelve years, I didn't feel like I was sinking. I felt sadness, sure. Anger? Maybe a little bit. But for the first time in more than a decade, I felt a little bit of that bitterness that's been protecting my heart melt away some. And I'm not sure what to do with that yet.

"I feel...I feel...I don't know yet. Give me a little more time," I say. Mom chuckles.

"Take your time, kiddo," she says.

"Listen," Dad says, and I can tell he's taken the phone, "do you need money?"

Ugh. That question weighs down on me.

Because, technically, I don't need money. I'm still getting money, *making* money, off my ex-husband. And there's such a dirty undertone to that.

I remember reading once that one of Paul McCartney's ex-wives fought for a shit-ton of his hard-earned Beatles money when they split up. And I remember feeling so disgusted. That was *his* money. She didn't earn it. He did.

And now, here I am.

Skating off of my ex-husband's hard-earned money like a teenager with an allowance.

I need to figure something out.

"Nah, I'm okay for now. I'm going to apply for a few jobs this week," I tell him.

"There, or here?" he asks. I swallow. There. Definitely there. I think.

"Okay, hon, call us later this week," Dad says. I say my goodbyes and hang up.

I take in a deep breath and lean back in the chair.

"Ya know, we could always use some extra help at the store," I hear his silky voice say as he rounds the corner of the porch and walks up the steps. I clear my throat and sit straight up.

"Uh, wh-what?" I ask.

"Sorry, didn't mean to eavesdrop; I just overheard the tail-end there," Ryder says, handing me a to-go coffee cup and a small paper bag. He sits on the rail directly in front of me.

"What's this?" I ask.

"Ah, stopped by Shirley's earlier today. She mentioned my 'friend' that was in town and told me to bring you this slice of pie," he says with a suspicious smile. I manage not to smile back and set the bag down on the arm of my chair.

"That's so nice," I say. "Thanks for bringing it."

"No problem," he says.

"What are you doing here?" I ask.

He shrugs and looks out over the water.

"I don't know," he says. "I guess I just didn't like the thought of you being up here alone."

I let out a sarcastic chuckle.

"I've been alone a lot over the last twelve years, and I've been just fine," I tell him. His head drops, then he slowly lifts his eyes to me.

"I missed a lot," he whispers, and my heart jumps an extra beat in my chest. I don't know what to say, so I just look down at the ground. "Do you...do you want to

39

come by my house for dinner tomorrow? I make a mean pork barbeque, and I have a big roast thawing that I can't possibly eat by myself."

I look up at him, and I feel a little tug at the corner of my lips.

"Tomorrow sounds good," I say, still avoiding fully smiling at him. Not on purpose, it's just this sinking, guilty feeling I get anytime I feel myself warming up to him.

But he doesn't hold back. He smiles at me—that same perfect smile I remember from so long ago. That same smile he gave me the first time he pulled me onto his boat. The same one he gave me when he first brought me into Lou's. The same one he gave me when he told me he would wait for me to finish school.

I remember him then, so vividly, the day I first laid eyes on him. When my whole world changed.

8

THEN, SUMMER BEFORE JUNIOR YEAR

"Kids, where are you?" Dad calls from the main level of the lake house. I'm lying out on the back deck, a towel draped over my face, trying to soak in the sun through every pore on my body.

We've been here for two weeks, and I'm starting to get bored.

Don't get me wrong, Meade Lake is my favorite place in the world. It brings me so much peace, so much calmness. Everything slows down, the food is amazing, the views are untouchable.

Walking out onto the balcony every morning while the sun trudges up over the tops of the mountains is like a dream.

But I'm sixteen. I need to *do* something.

Chase is non-stop when we're here. On the boat, in town, eating, working out, fishing. But I've noticed him slowing down a bit, too.

"I'm out here," I call, scooting off of the chaise lounge and wrapping a towel around me. I head inside and see Dad tying a tie in the mirror. Mom comes down the steps, looking less than pleased in a fitted dress and heels.

"Where are you all going?" Chase asks, his hair a floppy mess on the top of his head. He gives his head a shake, and suddenly, his eyes are visible.

"Tonight's the benefit back home, remember?" Dad asks. Oh, yeah. The summer benefit for Kelford that our parents go to every year. "Duty calls." As the mayor of a tiny Pennsylvania town, Dad actually stays pretty busy. He had humble beginnings, starting as a teacher, just like Mom.

But he wanted more. He didn't like the way the schools were structured. He didn't like the lack of empathy. He didn't like that some kids went without food. So he worked his way up through administration.

He became a principal then eventually moved on to the school board. When he saw other issues arising in town, he ran for mayor—and won.

It's been a busy few years, but it's been pretty cool.

Mom, however, still thinks she can make the most difference on the front lines, with the youth of our little town. She supports Dad in all he does, but she has made it clear, more than once, that his career will not get in the way of hers.

I love her for that.

But being a teacher means she's off for the summer. Dad is, too, for the most part, which is why we end up in Meade Lake all summer. To decompress. But there are a few little engagements here and there where he needs to show his face. Like tonight, for example.

"You look hot, Mom," I tell her as she fluffs her hair in the mirror. She rolls her eyes at me and smiles. Aside from a little more curve to her body, she and I are twins. Chocolate-brown hair that's board straight, matching brown eyes, and petite. We both tan in summer, as does Chase, but he has Dad's light-blue eyes.

I'm proud to look like my mom. I'm proud to be like her.

"We will be back late tonight," Dad tells us, grabbing his keys off the oak table by the front door. "Please don't burn the house down. And don't do anything stupid," he says, eyeing Chase. Chase holds his hands up in defense.

"Hey, why are you looking at me? She's the one who crashed the car last month!" he says, pointing to me.

"You're both still learning," Mom says. "And let's not forget who we caught trying to sneak Jenny Murphy into the house a few weeks ago."

I cross my arms and give him a "what now" look. He swallows.

"Seriously, you two, be safe and smart. I left some cash on the counter. We will call you when we're on our way back so you can put all the furniture back in place and kick everyone out of the big rager you're going to have," Mom says, kissing each of our heads. We laugh and say goodbye.

As if we know anyone up here to have a "rager."

As if I'd be interested in having a "rager." That's Chase's deal. Not mine.

We wave as they pull out of the gravel driveway and then head back in the house.

"Wanna do something?" I ask Chase.

"Like?"

"I don't know, fish?" I say. He shakes his head.

"Nah. I fished for hours yesterday. They're not biting

as much as last year. I'm gonna go into town. I met this girl at the coffee shop today. Luna," he says, his eyes sparkling like an idiot when he says her name.

"So?"

"So, I'm going to meet up with her and some friends at O'Murray's in a bit."

He pauses awkwardly then shrugs.

"You wanna come?"

I scoff because we both know the answer to that. I'm the introverted twin. He's the extrovert, the social butterfly, the man who says all the right things. Sort of like Dad. I'm a little dependent on Chase for a social life; I freely admit that.

But I was looking forward to some time with my brother.

"No, thanks," I say.

He shrugs again.

"Okay. What are you gonna do?" he asks.

"I'll figure it out."

After a few minutes of primping himself and spraying on some of Dad's cologne that in no way matches up with a night at a lakeside restaurant, Chase says goodbye and hops in Dad's truck.

I sigh as I watch him pull away, realizing that this is how our life will be. Him with the plans, me without.

I hate it because, without my brother, I feel like I'm drowning. He's the most important person in my life. And maybe it's because I don't know a life without him. Maybe it's because he can read my mind before I even formulate a thought. Sharing a womb will do that to you.

I sulk around to the side porch of the house, grab a rod and a tackle box, and make my way down to the lake. But after an hour with no bites, I realize that, once again, Chase was right. No bites. I slip my shoes on and start the walk down the street that our big ol' lake house sits on. At the front of the neighborhood sits a large pond. I plop down on the shore, slip my shoes off, bait my hook, and cast.

I watch my bobber moving up and down with the wind, but nothing again.

I sigh. Isn't this just a damn metaphor.

Behind me, I hear the rumbling of an engine that sounds to be as old as I am. A dirty, green pickup truck drives by then stops at the corner. Slowly, it reverses back to me, and I swallow.

The driver rolls down the window, which he has to do manually—it's like he's driving an antique—and I go from being nervous and skeptical to being dumbfounded and skeptical. Because he's gorgeous. He has shaggy brown hair that sticks out of the front and sides of his backwards baseball cap. I feel my tongue jut out to wet my bottom lip.

I want to smack myself.

Serial killers can be good-looking, you idiot.

I clear my throat.

"Ma'am?"

Ma'am? He looks like he's older than me. Ma'am? Really?

"Yeah?"

"You know how to fish?" he asks, and I feel my body stiffen. What an asshole. Just because I don't have a man with me? Just because I don't look like I'm from Meade Lake? He's assuming I can't *fish?*

I roll my eyes.

"Yes, random kid, but thank you for your unwanted misogynistic skepticism. I can even put the worm on the hook, too," I say, my voice dripping with sarcasm. I turn back to my rod, reel it in, and re-cast. I hear him chuckle behind me, then I hear the engine cut off as he pulls the truck over a bit. He closes the door and walks toward me, and my heart is thudding in my chest.

"Well, uh, do you know how to read?" he asks.

I whip my head to him.

"*What?*"

He smiles, and it's devastating. One of those smiles that can bring you to your knees. One of those smiles that makes you forget about everything, including the fact that he just insulted your intelligence.

He points a finger behind me, and I turn to see a big white sign.

THIS POND IS NOT STOCKED, it reads. I bite the inside of my cheek. I slowly turn around and reel my hook in, wrapping it around my rod. There's no fucking fish in this pond.

"Fucking great," I mutter, slamming the tackle box shut. He chuckles again, and it's so conflicting, because I want to both laugh with him and slam him into his truck.

"There's another pond up a little ways. If you want, I can show you?"

I pause and turn to him slowly. He doesn't *look* like a threat, but I guess they never do. I eye his truck, and he turns to me.

"Oh, we can walk," he says, sensing my nervousness. I think for a minute.

"Okay," I shrug.

"Cool," he says, grabbing a rod out of the back of his truck and falling in line next to me as we walk down the road. He reaches over after a few moments and takes the tackle box out of my hand. I let him. "I'm Ryder, by the way."

"Mila," I say, adjusting my grip on my rod.

"Mila," he repeats my name, and it sounds like silk rolling off his tongue. "It's nice to meet you. You in town for the week?"

I shake my head.

"The summer. My family has a house on Joan's Way. We come every summer," I say. His eyes brighten a little bit when he hears that, and it makes my stomach flip. "How about you?"

"Nah, I'm a local," he says with that damn smile. "Been in Meade Lake my whole life and probably won't ever leave."

I smile back.

"Lucky," I say. "It's my favorite place."

"Mine, too."

A few minutes later, we turn onto a wooded path, and then I see a big open pond. There's a bridge that leads to a gazebo on the water. It's beautiful. We cross the bridge, and he sets the tackle box down. He kicks his shoes off and sits down, letting his feet dangle off the edge. Then I do the same.

"So, Mila," he says after he casts, "tell me something about yourself that you don't normally tell people you just met."

I have a hook between my teeth, retying the line to it. I lift my eyes to him.

"Wha-what?" It catches me off-guard.

He looks at me out of the corner of his eye and smiles. I feel this warmness fall over me, like the feeling you get when you're in the comfort of your own home. You can lay out, as unladylike as you please, hair in a bun, socks that don't match. And no one cares.

That's how it feels right now.

"Uh," I say, thinking for a minute. I cast out and watch the line hit the water. "I guess…" My voice trails off. I'm hesitant, but I look to him and see those green eyes sparkling, waiting to learn something about me.

"Okay, ah…I think my dad had an affair last year."

I swallow. The smile runs from his face, and he cocks his head.

"Whoa," he says. I nod and turn back to the water.

Shit. That was too much. I can kiss this handsome stranger goodbye.

"I'm really sorry about that. That sucks," he says. "Are they still together?"

Hmm. Maybe not?

I nod.

"Oh, yeah. I think she knows about it, too. There was this one time, last year, when he said he had a meeting to go to. It was at a weird time. My mom left shortly after he did, and there was a lot of screaming when they got back. That night ended with my dad leaving and my mom crying in her room. Then, the next day, they didn't speak of it—or ever again, to my knowledge," I say with a shrug. There's this weird, healing, cathartic feeling talking about all of this. Because until this moment, I never have. Chase wasn't home that night. I watched it all unfold from the top of the stairs and the front window. And then I laugh at the fact that I've told this secret to a perfect stranger within the first hour of knowing him.

"What's funny?" he asks.

"I've just never told anyone about that night. Not even my brother," I say.

"You have a brother?"

"Yep. We're twins."

"Where's he today?" Ryder asks me.

"O'Murray's. Meeting some hot new babe he met this morning—Luna Something," I say with a hint of disdain. Ryder breaks out laughing. "What?"

"Luna Peake. She's been dating Daniel Thorpe for two years. I don't know your brother, but I don't think he has much of a chance," Ryder says with a laugh. I laugh, too. Man, how I wish I could be there to witness that.

"Okay," I say, finally gathering myself. "Now it's your turn. You tell me something."

He pauses for a moment, looking down at his hands and then out at the water.

"I'd like to sit with you at that pond you were at until we catch a fish," he says.

"But...that pond doesn't have fish," I say slowly as I start to catch his meaning. My cheeks flush, and my eyes drop to the ground.

"Exactly."

9

I'm blow-drying my hair in the mirror of my room and put on a few flicks of mascara. I have on a flowy tank with my favorite pair of jean shorts. If I remember correctly, these are the first pair of jean shorts that Ryder ever—ahem—got into.

Man, what a journey these shorts have been on.

I stop on the way and grab a bowl of pre-made fruit salad from Meade Market then continue along the way to Big Moon Drive.

Every time I pull up to this house, I feel warmth, and I feel nausea, all at the same time. I take in a deep breath and get out.

Just as I'm knocking on the front door, a truck I recognize pulls up in the driveway. Derrick's smiling face pops out.

The front door to the house opens just as Derrick is stepping up onto the porch.

"Well, what a coincidence! I just happened to be in the neighborhood with this bottle of wine, and you two look like you're about to have dinner, so…" Derrick says with his smile. I give Ryder a look.

"You're afraid to have dinner with me alone, huh?" I ask. Derrick busts out laughing as Ryder nervously brushes a hand through his hair.

"She caught you, dude," Derrick says, handing the wine to Ryder and walking inside. Ryder holds the door open for me, and I make my way in. The smell of the pine, the views from inside the foyer, it all brings back a sweeping wave of memories. He takes the fruit from me then stirs something on the stove. He flicks off the burner and turns back around.

"Dinner's up," he says.

We make our plates and head out to the back deck that overlooks the water.

"So," I say, once everyone is seated and eating, "Derrick, tell me what you're up to—aside from running a business."

"Eh, you know. Same ol', same ol'. Just spending a lot of time with Mama and Miss May. Remember her?"

I nod. May was a sweet older woman who was real good friends with Derrick's mom, Alma. She has a huge house on the north end of the lake and would always let us jump off her dock.

"How are they doing?"

"They're…alright. Time has been rough to a lot of us," he chuckles then takes a bite.

"And you?" I ask, turning to Ryder. He clears his throat and takes a swig of his beer.

"Ah, you know. Just working at the shop and Lou's when he needs me. Everything has remained relatively the same in Meade Lake," he says. I nod. Almost everything.

"What about you, Mila? I heard you got married, right?"

I clear my throat and take a sip of water. I declined the wine; I don't need my inhibitions to be lowered around Ryder.

"Divorced officially, about a week ago," I say matter-of-factly. Nothing like calling out the big, fat, divorced elephant in the room. Derrick nods, and Ryder doesn't seem to react.

"I'm sorry to hear that," he says. I shrug it off.

"Eh, things happen. Sometimes people aren't meant to be," I say, my eyes pointed at Ryder. "I'm sort of a believer in the idea that no one person is really meant for another." *We weren't meant to be.*

But he doesn't shy away from my glance; he just narrows his eyes back at me from across the table, and it sends a shiver down my spine.

"I don't know about all that, now," Derrick says with a chuckle. "Ryder and Maura? Man, those two were—"

Then something happens. My eyes shoot to Derrick, then to Ryder. Ryder is glaring at Derrick. Derrick swallows audibly.

"Shit, I'm sorry, man, I just…" Derrick says, putting a hand to his head. My eyes are still on Ryder's. Derrick excuses himself, and there's half of me that's screaming to go with him.

"Maura?" I ask, as if I have any right to know. He swallows, and his eyes trail up to the sky.

"She was my wife," he says.

I feel this pang in my chest. I'm feeling a lot of things I don't quite understand. I'm curious as to who she was, when they got married, what she was like. I want to know why we're using the past tense. And I want to understand why, how, after all these years, after a marriage of my own, I could possibly be a tiny bit jealous.

"Was?" I ask. He nods.

"She died four years ago."

My heart's beating in my chest so hard that I'm sure he can hear it.

"Oh, wow, Ryder," I say breathlessly. "I'm sorry. I had no idea."

He smiles.

"And I had no idea you had gotten divorced—or married, for that matter. But we both had a loss, and I'm sorry for yours, too."

I nod.

After a few more minutes, Derrick comes back outside to get his dishes.

"Well, now that I made it infinitely more awkward for everyone, I'm going to head over to Mama's. I'll see y'all later," he says, bending down to kiss my cheek and nodding his head at Ryder. "See you tomorrow, man."

I help gather the rest of the dishes, and Ryder and I make our way to the kitchen to wash them. Without thinking, I grab a towel off the oven handle. He washes, I dry.

I want to know what happened to her, but I feel like I need to ease into that. We're on a need-to-know basis right now, him and me.

"So," I say, and he looks over to me, "what was she like?"

The fact that Derrick mentioned that Ryder and Maura were meant to be somehow burns my insides. Because once upon a time, I thought Ryder and I were.

When I was sixteen, I would have told you I loved

him. When I was seventeen, I would have said he was my soul mate, the direct correlation to my being in this universe. We were cosmic.

But when I was eighteen, I would have said I hated him. I would have said I wished he had never been born so that I could selfishly spare the heartache he caused.

He smiles as he washes the salad bowl.

"She was amazing," he says. "She had this crazy zest for life. She was an artist. She could walk up to anybody and get them smiling."

I'm smiling just hearing about her.

"She sounds great," I say.

"How about your husband?" he asks. "Must have been a real dope to lose ya."

I look up at him, and he gives me this playful smile as if to say *takes one to know one*.

I smile back at him, and I feel my cheeks flush.

I think about Luke. He was my light, my laugh, my home.

"He's...he's incredible, actually. He didn't lose me. Actually, I think I lost him," I say matter-of-factly. It feels weird to divulge this to him, but Ryder has a way of getting the information that should make me feel the most vulnerable and turning it on its head to make me feel stronger than before.

He nods, and I feel the air between us get a little bit cooler. We finish up, and I dry my hands on the towel and hang it back up.

"Well, thanks for dinner," I say, grabbing my keys off the counter.

"Hang on there," he says, leaning back against the counter. The way his arm muscles bulge when he crosses them over his chest makes me look away. "Don't I get a letter tonight?"

Oof. Given the nature of tonight's conversation, I was going to hold back tonight.

"We can do it another time, if you want," I say with a shrug. He smiles and takes a step closer to me. I look up at him, and I have this urge to get closer.

"I like that there's going to be 'another time,'" he says, "but I think I can handle one tonight. Even though they aren't the, ah, most pleasant things to read, I kinda like getting a little glimpse of the Mila I missed out on."

I smile and bend down to grab my book out of my bag that sits on the floor. As I stand, I feel his eyes on me, scanning me, and I love the way I feel under his gaze.

I turn around, open my journal, and flip to the next entry I had saved for him. I tear it out and hand it over.

Ryder,

I met a guy tonight. And I have this weird feeling about him.

It's sort of like the feeling I had when you first told me you liked me. Except that now I'm twenty-one, and it's a little bit more grown-up. We were both at a friend's house off-campus for a small get-together. Everyone else got drunk, but we stayed out on the patio all night just talking.

He's supposed to call me tomorrow. He was sweet, and kind, and funny. Like you.

. . .

*I REALLY LIKED HIM. I really **LIKE** him. But for some idiotic reason, when he went to kiss me goodnight, I half-expected you to be standing there when I opened my eyes.*

AND I HATE THAT.
Mila

I WATCH his eyes scan over the letter, and I see the pain beneath them rising to the top. He reads it again and then looks up to me.

"Is this the guy?" he asks. I nod.

"Yeah. Luke," I say. I look down at my pad then rip out the next letter.

"Two-for-one?" he says with a smile. I look down at the letter in my hand, and it starts to shake. The nerves. This one cuts me open like a damn knife. And the worst part is, I know it'll do the same to him, too. I hand it over.

RYDER,

IT'S MY WEDDING DAY. I'm literally sitting in the bridal suite. I've got my hair done, my makeup on, my dress is zipped. I've got a million and one people around me, and all I can do is think about my brother. And how he's supposed to be here, walking me down the aisle.

. . .

WHEN I WAS SIXTEEN, I thought he'd lead me down the aisle to you. You two would do that weird bro-hug thing you always did, and he'd probably tell you some inappropriate joke at the altar.

But neither of you are here.

AND NOW I have this amazing man waiting for me inside this church, smiling, thinking about all that our future holds. Waiting to tell me I'm the most beautiful woman he's ever seen.

And he has no idea that I'm sitting here thinking about you.

HOW BADLY I wish I wasn't.

Mila

HE FOLDS the note up and sticks it in his back pocket. He takes another step closer to me, and I hold my breath. I remember how intoxicating his scent used to be to me. There's no room for that right now.

"Oh, Mila," he whispers. "I know you were the most beautiful bride."

I lift my eyes to his slowly, and I can feel that familiar weakness, my senses going numb to the situation around me. I take a step back.

"Goodnight, Ryder," I say.

10

I'm lying in my bed at the inn, staring up at the ceiling. There's dark-green-and-red striped wallpaper everywhere, and it's making me dizzy. I'm so concentrated on it that I can't sleep. Or maybe I can't sleep because, earlier tonight, I wanted to kiss Ryder Casey.

The guy who killed my brother.

Jesus, I think I need to get laid or something.

And *not* by Ryder. Just in general. He shouldn't have this much power over me after all this time. He shouldn't be able to make me forget so easily.

I roll over and close my eyes, hoping that his face isn't the last one I see before I actually doze off.

THE NEXT MORNING, I'm up with the sun again. I drive into town and stop in at a little coffee shop. It must be new-ish to Meade Lake. It wasn't here when we were still coming.

"That'll be seven-oh-six," the barista says to me. As I

reach into my wallet and pull out my debit card, I stare down at the name.

Mila Boughman.

Boughman. As in, Luke Boughman's wife.

Ex-wife.

I pay for the coffee and donut I got and walk outside. I hear laughing and cheering up the street a little ways, and it's coming from Big Moon Sports.

I remember what he told me—that they were always looking for workers.

I don't have to go home at any certain time.

I could suck it up and eventually stay in the lake house so that I don't need to use Luke's money to pay rent.

I could stay in Meade Lake for a while, if I wanted.

But do I?

I walk down Lakeside Highway and cross the street at a crosswalk.

The store is huge with big windows that look out over the water. There are rafts and tubes displayed outside and even more hanging on the walls inside. There's a huge line wrapped around the inside of the store with people waiting to check out, but no one seems pushy or in a rush. Some people are looking through the clothing racks; others are checking price tags on sunglasses. Ryder is at the front desk, handling the massive crowd with ease. He's smiling and talking to the customers, offering restaurant recommendations to the vacationers for later. I slip around to the side of the desk where I see a sign that reads *Applications*. I snag one and a pen from the cup next to it then slink to the back of the store.

I take a breath as I fill it out. I haven't applied for a

job in a long time. I was with my last company for almost eight years, working in the accounts payable department. But then it got stale. I wasn't feeling fulfilled. I was losing my love for numbers. So I left and didn't look back.

I fill it out and turn back to the front of the store. As I make my way back up, I notice a slew of teenage girls patiently waiting for Ryder to give them the safety run-down of using kayaks. They each have on a different neon-colored bikini top, their hair with those perfectly tousled summer waves. They are batting their eyes and leaning further than necessary across the counter in his direction.

"Once we're done here, you'll take this slip down to the dock across the street, and Derrick will get you fitted for a life vest," he tells them.

"Oh, you don't do that here?" one asks while the others giggle around her. I can't even blame them. When I was their age, Ryder was all I saw, too.

I clear my throat behind them, and they whip their heads around to me. They straighten up like they've been caught. Ryder smiles.

"Hey," he says to me, and it's like no one else in the store even exists.

"Hey," I say back. "Sorry, didn't mean to interrupt."

"Nope, we're all good here. Here's your slip, ladies. Enjoy!"

They shoot me the stink eye as they walk past, and I can't help but smile.

"Quite the fan club," I say with a chuckle, but he smiles and shrugs it off.

"So, what can I do for you today, ma'am?" he asks, leaning across the counter on his elbows.

I slap the application down on the counter between us. He looks down at it, registers what it is, then looks back up to me.

"You're hired," he says, one corner of his lips tugged up into the most perfect half-smile.

"You're not even gonna check my experience? Call a reference?" I ask, smiling playfully back at him. He shakes his head.

"Nah. I knew a girl like you once. If you're anything like her, I think you're good," he says. My smile fades a little bit. I don't know if I'm really anything like that girl he used to know.

Finally, the rest of the crowd in the store disperses for a bit, and it's just him and me.

"If you want, I can show you the ropes," he says. I nod. He walks me around, showing me where everything goes. He walks me to the counter again and explains the check-out process, the different rental packages, and how much everything costs.

Then, we walk up the big staircase toward the back-side of the store, and he walks me inside a massive storage room filled with boxes, and plastic, and tubes, and paddles.

"Whoa," I say.

"Yeah. It's a mess in here," he says. "But this is where we have all our stock of everything. We try to take inventory once a week."

I nod.

"Got it," I say.

"After the lunch rush comes and goes, Derrick and I will switch, and I'll go down to the docks. You can join me, and I can show you how everything down there works."

I nod again.

We're walking around the store, tidying things up, and then another big crowd of people comes bursting in the doors. Rental times are three-hour shifts, so Ryder explained that they come and go like this throughout the day. Finally, the crowd dissipates again, and Derrick comes up from the water.

"Hey!" he says.

"Meet our new employee," Ryder says, not lifting his head from the paperwork he's filing. Derrick looks at me, eyebrows knit together.

"What?" he asks. I smile and shrug.

"I'm around for a little while," I tell him.

"Or maybe longer," Ryder says from the counter, and we both turn to him. His eyes are wide, and I realize he didn't mean to say it out loud. We don't say anything; we just stare at each other for a moment. Derrick clears his throat and walks to the front.

"Well, I can take over up here," he says, and Ryder nods.

"Cool, I'll show her the ropes down there."

I follow him out the doors and across the street to a big set of rickety wooden stairs. If I took one misstep—which I am prone to doing—I'd be face first into the lake.

There's a big dock with a shed at the end of it. Inside is a rack of life vests, all varying in size, and a few file folders.

"So, here's where we collect their payslips, see what they're renting, and hand out the life vests," he says. I nod. This is really a well-oiled machine he and Derrick are running here. In another life, I think I'd be really proud of him.

Maybe I'm a little proud of him in this life, too.

"To make sure they have the right size, have them try it on." He looks at me and holds one up. "May I?" he asks.

It takes me a moment to realize he wants to put one on me. I pull my hair up in a bun and nod.

I slip my arms through the holes and zip it in front. Then, he reaches over and tugs the zipper up.

"Make sure the zipper is all the way up and all three clips are secure," he says. I nod. "Then, grab the shoulder straps and give a little tug upwards. If the straps go past their ears, it's too big."

We both freeze for a moment, realizing how close we are. The shed smells like lake water and sunblock, but his scent is the only thing I can concentrate on. The shed rocks with a big wake, and we stumble a bit. He steadies me, and our eyes meet.

"Got it," I finally say.

A few people come down with their slips, and I help Ryder find the right sizes for them. Out on the dock sit two chairs. As we walk toward them, a flock of jet skis fly by us, sending another huge wake our way. Before I manage to reach my chair, I'm wobbling. No, wait.

I'm falling.

Off the dock.

Into the water.

I pop my head up out of the water, looking around. Ryder is right in front of me, his arm lowered down into the water.

"You okay?" he asks. I swim up to the side of the dock and grab hold of him. With one quick movement, he pulls me up and back onto the dock. I nod and start to laugh. He does too, until he looks down and quickly stops. He looks away, his cheeks flushing with red.

I look down, and suddenly I want to jump back in the water and never come out.

Because of course I wore a white tank top.

Without thinking, he grabs my arm and pulls me across the dock into the shed. He closes the door behind us and turns around. He lifts the bottom of his blue Big Moon Sports polo up over his head and hands it to me.

"Here," he says. My eyes scan his body quickly, soaking it all in. There was a time when I could picture it from memory, every freckle, every peak and valley of his muscles. Now they're bigger, firmer. I remember kissing his chest and neck, inhaling so deeply in hopes of carrying him with me everywhere I went.

I remember crashing into him, fists full of rage and pain and love and lust, pounding against him.

I take the shirt, and he slips quietly out the door, like the gentleman he's always been, leaving me to change in privacy.

I slip my wet shirt up off over my head then pull his on. It's warm against my cool body, and I steady myself as his scent wraps around me.

I walk back out, rolling the bottom of the huge shirt up a little bit.

"Looks better on you, anyway," he says with a smile as he waves a boat renter in.

"Thanks for this," I say. "I'll wash it and bring it back."

He smiles.

"No worries," he says. "I have a million of those. I'll have Derrick throw me down a new one once this crowd gets back in." I nod. "So, you're gonna be here for a little while?"

I look at him, and I can see the hope in his eyes.

I don't know what he wants from me; it's not like he's waited for me all these years. But maybe it's that he wants to be forgiven as badly as I want to forgive him.

"Yeah, I think so. Open-ended, I guess," I say.

"Cool, well, promise you'll give me two weeks' notice?" he says with a smile. I smile and nod.

"Promise."

11

THEN, SUMMER BEFORE JUNIOR YEAR

A few hours of fishing pass, and I've caught three sunfish. Ryder helped me free them, and then we celebrate when he catches a bass. He tosses it back and rises to his feet.

"You wanna head into town? We could meet up with your brother," he says. I look up at him. The sun is starting to go down now, but I don't want this day to end.

"And watch him fall on his ass with that girl? Sure," I say. He laughs and pulls me up to him. He grabs my pole and the tackle box, and we start back down the path toward his truck.

"That was fun," I say, thinking out loud. He smiles down at me.

"Well, we have all summer," he says with a shrug.

"All summer," I say, counting down the days that we still have left. This morning, I was almost hoping for time to pass. Now, I want it to slow down so that we're in Meade Lake as long as possible.

. . .

WE DRIVE TO O'MURRAY'S, and before I can even get out, Ryder's on my side of the truck, opening the door. He helps me down, and we walk in stride together down the steps and onto the restaurant patio.

"Casey!" a voice calls from the back corner. A group of kids that all appear to be around our age are waving in our direction.

"Ryder Casey, where you been?" says one, a handsome black guy perched up on the patio railing.

On the side of the group sits a pouting Chase. In the middle of the group sits a beautiful girl, perched between the legs of another one of the guys, smiling up at him like he holds the whole world there.

"Hey, Luna, hey Daniel," Ryder says.

"Hey," they say back in unison. I almost laugh. Chase is used to being the big man on campus at home. Looks like he just struck out.

But he perks up when he sees me, and I brace myself for his reaction.

"Hey, guys, this is Mila," he says, holding a hand out to me. I step forward, and he places it on the small of my back. I feel my whole body tense under his touch.

"Hi," I mutter, tucking a piece of hair behind my ear.

"We were fishing," he says.

"Fishing?" Chase asks, stepping forward.

"You know her?" one of the other girls asks. Chase nods.

"She's my twin sister," he says. They all look to me.

"How'd you get caught up with Ryder, here?" Luna asks. I look up at him.

"Yeah. How *did* you get caught up with Ryder, here?" Chase asks, his arms crossing over his chest. He takes a step toward us, but Ryder doesn't flinch. Doesn't even bat an eye. He just smiles.

"Saw her fishin' at the pond at the corner of Rainweather and Joan's Way."

"But...that pond isn't stocked," Daniel says. Ryder looks down at me, and we exchange a smile.

"I know that now," I say, never taking my eyes off him.

"Well, come, sit. We just ordered. I'll call Kirby over. She's our waitress tonight," Luna says, waving her down.

They pull up chairs for us, but to my dismay, Chase snags the chair next to me, booting Ryder out of the way. I watch him, but again, he doesn't flinch. He just smiles, happily grabbing the chair next to him.

We laugh, talk, and they ask us where we're from, how long we've been coming to Meade Lake, which of us is older, if we get along, if we can read each other's minds.

"Do you guys, like, date each other's friends and stuff?" the cute black guy asks, and I learn that his name is Derrick. Chase and I look at each other, and he looks down at his plate.

"He dates mine," I say so that he doesn't have to.

It's no secret that when it comes to dating, Chase has got the experience. Not me.

Chase's eyes flash to Ryder.

"I've been trying to set her up with my buddy Todd," he says, leaning back in his chair.

Fuck off, Chase.

Ryder swallows and leans back in his own.

"They've known each other for years. But she won't budge," Chase says. Ryder leans forward in his seat.

"Maybe he's just not the right match for her, then," he says matter-of-factly. Then he leans back again, his eyes trained on mine.

When we're finished, the group starts dispersing to their cars and boats. Ryder takes my hand and pulls me to him.

"Can I drive you home?" he asks.

"It's cool. I got her," Chase says, walking toward us. I roll my eyes. Ryder smiles down at me.

"He's just doing what any good brother would do," he says.

"Oh yeah? Being a pain in the ass?" I say, crossing my arms as Chase walks to the truck. Ryder laughs, and it makes my stomach flip.

"No. Making sure that the guy who's into his sister is fit for her," he says. I look up at him.

"Into me, huh?"

"Yeah, Mila. Into you." He takes a step closer to me and takes my hand in his again. "Can I see you again this week?"

I smile and nod, giving his hand a squeeze.

"Sure. And maybe the one after that. I've got eight more to spend here," I tell him. He smiles.

"Then let's make 'em count." I nod and skip away back to the truck where Chase is continuing to pout in the driver's seat.

I put on my seatbelt as he speeds off.

"Slow down, you idiot," I tell him. He lays off the gas a bit, but he's got anger all over his face. "What's your deal?"

"Nothing."

I pause and turn to him, waiting for him to come clean. We shared a room, but sometimes, it feels like we share a brain. I can't *actually* read his mind, but sometimes, it feels like I can.

"That guy, he just rubs me the wrong way," he says. I roll my eyes and turn to look out the window.

"Oh, stop it, Chase," I say.

"I mean it," he says. "I don't like him."

I turn back to him.

"Are you sure this has nothing to do with the fact that I got a teeny-tiny bit of action today, and you didn't?"

Chase's head whips to mine as the car weaves with it then straightens back up. "Jesus, Chase. Pay attention to the fucking road."

"What *action?*" he asks. I roll my eyes and can't help but stifle a laugh.

"Not *action* in the sense that *you* would get action. But just that someone's actually interested in me rather than you."

Chase's eyes are filled with emotion, but I can't make out just what it is. He stares ahead at the road, and for the rest of the drive, he doesn't say a word. His grip is tight on the steering wheel, making his knuckles big and white. When we get out and walk up the porch steps, he stops and turns to me.

"You're more of a catch than you give yourself credit for, you know that?" he says to me. I turn to him.

"What are you talking about?"

"I mean, you have a lot to offer. Guys ask me about you a lot," he says. My eyebrows shoot up.

"They do?"

"Yeah, they do. But I always warn them that you're special. I don't, like, forbid them from trying or anything. I just warn them that they should make sure they aren't hitting out of their league." I swallow and look up at him.

"Chase, I…"

"It always bothers me a little bit, just because you're my sister, and anything that could potentially hurt you is a no-go for me. But at least with the guys back home, I know them. I can find them. I can hunt them down, if need be."

I laugh, but his face stays serious.

"I don't know this guy. You hardly do, either. I don't like it. I feel out of control," he admits. I reach up and punch his shoulder playfully.

"Ya know, I *am* a full three minutes older than you," I tell him, "which makes me your big sister, technically. You don't always have to worry about me. I can handle more than you give me credit for."

He smiles and nods.

"And you know something else, C? You can't always be there for me to work out things like this. I know it's not your fault. I know I always put you in that spot of making you be my hero. But you can't always be that for me."

His eyes look full and sad, and it breaks my heart a little.

"Is it because you want *him* to be your hero?" he asks, giving me a playful nudge. I think for a moment.

"Nah. It's because sometimes I need to be my own."

He nods and takes a seat on the porch. I sit down next to him. We look up at the sky. The moon is so much brighter here in Meade Lake, like the water and the mountains magnify it.

Suddenly, a chuckle escapes his lips.

"What?" I ask him.

"Just thinkin'. What if that guy is, like, *the one?* Someday we could all be dancing at your wedding," he says, shaking his head.

I laugh and give him another shove.

"I just met him. And we're sixteen," I say. Chase shrugs.

"You gotta start somewhere."

12

I've worked six shifts now at Big Moon Sports, and I feel like I'm getting the hang of it. It's still a little stressful when the lunch crowd comes in to get their rentals, but I'm starting to move faster now that I know what I'm doing.

But whenever a group of females comes in, be it a bachelorette party or something, and bats their eyes in Ryder's direction, I always find myself on the other side of the counter, offering to register them so he doesn't have to.

He smiles and happily takes the help, and I'm left feeling like I've somehow protected him—or maybe, protected myself.

We've been working well together—him, Derrick, and I. Sometimes Ryder takes later shifts for Lou, so I offer to close up. Other days, he can't work till the afternoon because he's doing yard work, so it's just Derrick and me. But sometimes, Derrick has a day off, and it's just me and Ryder. Those are becoming my favorite days, and I need to remind myself, again, why I'm here.

I need to remind myself that I can't—won't—fall back to where we were pre-Chase. It's not healthy; it's not plausible. It's not *real*. I need to figure out how to move on with my life without the heavy weight of Ryder Casey hanging over me. But the longer I'm here in Meade Lake, the longer I want to lie there and let it suffocate me.

"Hey," he says, nudging me behind the counter as I file away the last of the day's paperwork. "You got dinner plans?"

I swallow and shake my head.

"I'm gonna pick up some Linda's on my way back," he says. "Want some pizza?"

I smile and nod.

"Man, I can't believe I've been up here for three weeks and have yet to have a slice," I say. "That sounds good." He smiles.

"Cool. I'll meet you back at my place in about twenty?"

I smile and nod.

"Oh, and here's your first paycheck," he says, sliding an envelope across the counter to me. I grab it and thank him then hop in my car and head back to the inn.

I hurriedly open the envelope when I park and flip the check over.

I almost want to laugh at the amount.

It's not a large amount, by any means. And if I want to continue staying up here, I'm either going to need something else, or I'm going to need to check out of this expensive-as-shit inn. I'm done living off of Luke.

I pull my phone out of my bag and pull up his contact. I suck in a deep breath and press it.

"Hello?" he answers on the second ring, his voice breathy and unstable.

"Hi, Luke," I say.

"Mila," he says, his voice full of what sounds like hope. I swallow the lump in my throat that rises every time I think of him. Think of how I let him down.

"Listen, uh, I want to call the lawyers and permanently end the alimony agreement."

There's a long pause over the phone.

"You...you what?"

"I got a job, actually. And I just don't feel right taking it anymore. Thank you so much, really. But I can't live off of you forever."

I hear him sigh on the other end. I picture him in our house, his face pressed against his hand.

"Mila, I'll be there for you, however you need, for as long as you need," he promises. This time I blink out a tear.

"I can't let you anymore, Luke. I've gotta go. Goodnight," I say, clicking the "end" button.

I walk into the inn and up to the front desk where Mrs. Miller is flipping through the pages of a magazine.

"Excuse me, ma'am? I need to check out," I tell her. She looks up at me over the rim of her glasses.

"Aww, sad to see your stay in Meade Lake coming to an end," she says as I hand her my card.

It's not over.

I go back up to my room and grab my bag, throwing everything inside it. I throw it in the back of my car after running a brush through my hair one more time in the mirror.

I know where I'll go tonight after I leave Ryder's.

And I know it'll kill me.

. . .

I GET BACK on the road and drive the few miles to Big Moon Drive. I changed out of his shirt—although, I won't lie and say that peeling it off my body didn't do something to me. When I pull in, he's getting out of his own truck with the pizzas in hand.

"Good timing," he says, unlocking the front door and holding it open for me to go first. Always the gentleman.

"Thanks," I say. "Can I give you some money for those?"

He shoots me a look. I smile and nod. We both know the answer to that one.

When we get inside, I walk to the cabinet without thinking and grab two plates and two glasses, and then I grab a few napkins from the table. When I turn back around, he's smiling at me.

"What?"

"Nothin'. I guess I just like that you know your way around here," he says. I swallow and feel my cheeks flush. I didn't even realize it until right now, how at home I feel here in this house. The house we spent so much time in. The house I know he ran away to when his parents would fight. The house we spent so much unsupervised time in when Aunt Winnie was off again on one of her adventures.

"Sorry, I guess I just—"

"Don't apologize," he says, stepping extra close to me and taking the plates from my hands, letting his fingers linger on mine for a moment too long. I clear my throat and nod as I follow him into the dining room.

The room is flooded with pink and orange light from what's left of the sun in the sky.

"God," I say between bites of cheesy goodness, "I forgot about this." I nod toward the sunset that's taking my breath away. He smiles and looks over to me.

"Yeah," he says. "I forgot about them with you."

I look at him and involuntarily smile at him.

Don't do it. Don't fall for him, Mila.

A few minutes later, the two of us have gone through four beers and one-and-a-half large pizzas. I sit back in the chair and put a hand on my stuffed gut.

"Man, there is really nothing like Brenda's pizza," I say. He smiles and leans back in his own chair.

"Nope, nothing," he says.

"Can I use your bathroom?" I ask. He nods, grabbing our plates from the table and heading to the sink.

"Course," he says.

I hop up from the table and head down the long cedar-lined hallway. I love this house. It's not the biggest house on the lake, but to me, it always felt like home. That is, till I reach the end of the hall. I can't remember which door the bathroom is, and it bugs me.

I reach for the knob on the second door on my right, and I freeze.

I open to a room with walls that are painted pink.

A purple comforter drapes off the tiny bed in the corner of the room.

Floral curtains hang from the windows, and a rocking horse sits in another corner, right next to a tiny bookshelf.

A princess costume lies on the floor in a bunch, complete with tiny heels and a tiara.

"Shit," I hear him whisper as he makes his way

down the hall to me. Quickly, he reaches around me to grab the door and close it, as if it would erase what I've just seen.

"What...what was that?"

He hangs his head, bringing his hands to his face. He walks past me, head still in hand.

"Shit," he mutters again to himself. I follow close behind.

"Ryder?"

His shoulder flinches a little with the sound of my voice, and he turns to me slowly.

He lets out a long breath.

"That was my daughter's room," he says. I feel my chest heave up and down a few times. He looks down at me with wide, heavy eyes, waiting for my response. The truth is, I'm waiting for it, too.

I walk past him like a zombie, blinking wildly. I reach for my beer and take a long sip, then I tilt my head back and guzzle the rest of it. I put the bottle back down on the counter, then I turn and walk back to the living room. I plop down on the couch, and he carefully sits next to me.

I swallow my initial shock, letting it sink in. Then I turn to him.

"You have a kid?"

He nods.

"Yeah."

"How...how old is she?"

"Almost four," he says. I blink, trying to do the math. He said his wife died four years ago.

"Did your wife...?" I start to ask. He just nods.

"Yeah. She died in childbirth. She hemorrhaged,

and they couldn't stop the bleeding," he says. I gasp and cover my mouth.

"Oh, God. I'm so sorry, Ryder," I say. Because I am. I can't even imagine. He gives me a sad smile then scoots his hand toward mine on the couch, careful not to actually touch me.

"I appreciate that, but you're the last person who should say sorry to me," he says. I swallow.

"What's her name?" I ask.

"Annabelle," he tells me. Then his whole being lights up. From his eyes to his feet, it's like his whole body is lighter now. "She's everything." I smile and nod.

I wonder, whole-heartedly, what it's like to have another being, another person, that part of you actually made up. That has traits of you and someone you loved. That has your nose or your partner's lips. That makes you smile just by growing. That truly becomes *everything*.

"Where is she?" I ask.

"She stays with Derrick's mom, Alma, on nights that I work. And sometimes, May and her granddaughter take her if I have to grab a shift at Lou's or something. These people are totally helping me raise her," he says matter-of-factly, but he doesn't seem upset by it. He seems grateful. "I was so, so lost when we first got home from the hospital. I had never even changed a damn diaper," he says with a sad chuckle. "Alma came over, Derrick brought food, and his brother and sister made us frozen meals. May sent over bags and bags of clothes for her from her granddaughter. Lou refused to put me on the schedule, but I somehow still got a paycheck every two weeks while I was home with her. Derrick took over every shift at the store, and somehow, I still got my cut from that, too. These people, I tell you."

I smile. He goes on.

"After everything, my mom went back to California. Still with no option to go with her. For a while I wanted to get away, which was scary. I had never wanted to leave this place. But it was pretty painful just looking around. But then, these people, they lifted me up, ya know? They sorta…brought me back."

"That's amazing," I say.

"I was going to pick Annabelle up tonight, but Alma called and said she fell asleep early, so she is keeping her tonight."

I nod again, and then the air grows thick and quiet.

"Mila, I didn't tell you about her because I didn't want to add anything more complicated than what you came here for. And I'm also really particular about who I bring around her," he says. I look up at him and cock my head.

"Don't get me wrong," he goes on, "I'd love for her to meet you. But I try to avoid her meeting people who might be leaving soon. She gets attached, and she doesn't even know it yet, but she's already been through such a major loss."

"That makes sense," I say. "I'd love to meet her. But I just don't know how long…"

His eyes drop to his lap, and he nods.

"I know," he whispers. "When you figure it out, let me know. No pressure."

I nod, but we both know I'm putting enough pressure on myself for the both of us.

I PULL into the driveway of 114 Joan's Way, where our big ol' lake house sits at the back of a perfect cove.

Nestled at the base of Sundance Mountain, with breathtaking views of Meade Lake and a private dock, the website description reads. The rental company tells my parents that it's one of the most popular properties, but when I told my parents I was coming up here, my dad canceled all rentals until further notice.

I get out and stare up at it, the moon shining on it like a spotlight. I walk up the front porch and fiddle with my keychain. I unlock the big oak door and push it open.

It smells like cleaner. It doesn't smell like pine and whatever food my mother used to cook for us while we played in the water all day.

The furniture is rearranged, and everything feels out of place. I carry my bags inside and drop them inside the door. I throw my keys onto the front table, only to hear them crash to the floor. When I look over, I realize the front table has been moved across the room.

I sigh.

I get to work moving the front table back to its rightful spot. I switch the loveseat from the right corner where it sits now to the left corner where it's supposed to be. The only thing wrong now is that the couch is at a weird angle. I try my best to move it, even taking a running start, but it's not budging. I let out a long breath.

Fine. That'll wait for another day.

I walk up the big wooden steps to the bedrooms. I peek into my parents' room. Everything looks the same, the big king bed in the center, the skylight flooding the room with starlight.

I walk down the hall to my room and open the door.

Even the comforter is the same, a pale green my mother had picked out when I was just a kid.

I walk out into the hall and slowly push open the bedroom door next to mine.

His room.

Everything appears to be in its rightful place, but nothing feels right.

13

The next morning, I'm up early, my neck stiff from having fallen asleep on the couch that's in the wrong spot.

I have the day shift this morning, and for some reason, today, I can't wait to get to work.

I pull on a pair of jean shorts and my own blue polo then hop in my car and head down to the store.

When I pull in and look around, though, I don't see Ryder's truck, and I'm surprised when I'm overcome with disappointment.

Inside, Derrick is pulling out some new forms from the drawer under the cash register and tidying up the counter.

"Hey," I say, slinging my bag over the counter and tucking it underneath.

"Morning," he says.

"Where's Ryder?" I ask.

"He got called into Lou's tonight, so we switched shifts today. You're stuck with me; sorry," he says with a playful smile. I scrunch my nose and smile back at him.

"Did he tell you that I...found out? About...Annabelle?"

He smiles, never lifting his eyes from the counter.

"He told me," he says. Slowly, he looks up at me. "I told you; he's been through a lot."

I nod.

"It sounds like it," I say.

"For what it's worth," he says, "and it may be worth nothing, but it's doing him good that you're here."

My eyes widen.

"He needs you to forgive him as much as you need to do it," he says before disappearing behind me and into the back of the store.

THE SHIFT SEEMS to drag on today, even though we're busy as a mother. I'm checking people in and out, switching with Derrick down at the docks, and finally, it's closing time. The sun is disappearing, and the last of our renters are coming back in.

Finally, I check the last person back in and lock up the shed.

As Derrick and I are walking out to our cars, I stop him.

"Does your mom have Annabelle today?" I ask.

He looks down at his phone.

"Ryder's shift is at eight; he usually drops her off a little earlier so she can have dinner. She should be there now." I nod.

"Thanks."

I get in my car, and before I realize it, I'm auto-piloting toward Big Moon Drive. This is the first day since I've been in Meade Lake that I haven't seen him, and it feels...off.

I turn into the driveway and hop out, knocking on the door in a hurried fashion. In a moment's time, he opens it.

"Mila?" he asks, confused. "You okay?"

"Yeah," I say, stumbling over what to tell him next.

"Do you...do you need something?" he asks. I want to kick myself. Why did I come? Why did I do this to myself?

"I...I, uh," I start to mumble, and I can see he wants to save me from myself.

"I'm just getting ready for my shift at Lou's. Wanna come in for a bit?" he asks. I nod and step inside.

"Did you eat yet? I have some leftovers," he calls from down the hall in his room.

"I'll grab something on my way back to the house," I say, leaning up against the counter. I look around. He keeps this place spotless, which I imagine has to be hard to do with an almost-four-year-old.

"How was being back at the house?" he calls.

"It was...different," I call back.

"I'm sure," he says.

I walk down the side of the big island in the middle of the kitchen and turn around the corner, passing his keys, his phone, and a pile of mail.

But I pause when I see an envelope on the top addressed to Ryder.

The return address reads: R.H. Oncology Associates.

I hear blood rushing through my ears, and I feel my breathing quicken. The envelope is shaking in my fingers when he appears from down the hall.

"Did you want to come—" he starts but freezes when he sees me. Instantly, he knows something is wrong.

His eyes trail down to my hand, the envelope turned up toward him. He lifts them to me slowly.

"What…is this?" I ask, although, I probably shouldn't. It's not my place. I'm here for one reason and one reason only. I should have just pretended I didn't see it. But I can't, because my heart feels like it's beating in my throat, and I think I'm going to faint.

"Mila," he whispers, stepping toward me slowly. I take a step back, and my knees feel a little weak. I stumble, and he lunges forward to steady me. His fingers are wrapped around my biceps, and I force myself to look up at him. "You okay?" he asks.

I nod.

"Ryder, what is this?"

He swallows and nods for me to sit down on the couch again. I need to stop coming to his house. I keep finding out his deepest, darkest secrets, and I don't think I can handle any more.

"So, two years before we had Annabelle, I had this…episode. Maura and I were walking down by the water, and I just dropped to the ground and froze."

My eyes are wide, but I can feel my heart starting to close itself off.

"She called 911, and I ended up in the hospital for a few days. After a million scans, it ended up that I had a small brain tumor. It had caused the seizure."

I can't speak. I just stare at him.

"I had surgery, did some treatment, all was well, and a year later, it was like I was a new man. Maura and I got married on top of the mountain the day after my last treatment. Another year later, I lost Maura. But I found the love of my life in the form of that little girl."

My heart melts a little with the way he talks about his daughter.

"So...you're okay now?" I ask. He swallows.

"For the most part. I've been having some trouble with my vision that's been making driving at night a little difficult. I'm sure everything is fine, but I made an appointment and got some scans done just to be safe. A few came back abnormal."

"Abnormal?" I ask, unable to fully hide the panic in my voice.

"Yeah. So I have an appointment this week to get the results," he says. We're silent for a moment as I digest everything he's told me.

Jesus. When Derrick said he'd been through some shit, I didn't know the half of it.

Another moment passes, and he leans across the couch, placing his hands on mine as they pull at the tag on the pillow I didn't even know I was squeezing.

"Hey," he says, "are you...are you worried about me?"

My eyes flick up to his. I don't answer him with words. I don't have to. Even after all these years.

"Mila, I'm okay, okay?" he says. I nod. "Please don't... Please don't let this add to any stress you already have or make you feel like you can't do what you came here to do. I'm sure I'm fine anyway, and you need to do your own healing." He lets his hands rest on mine for a moment longer then stands. "I have to head up to Lou's. Do you wanna come hang out for a bit?"

I think for a moment then shake my head. I just

want to go back to the lake house and decompress. He nods, grabs his keys, and we walk back out to our cars.

"Hey," he says before turning to his, "I haven't gotten a letter in a few days." His lips curve into a smile. I nod and walk to my car, opening the door and pulling the journal out of my bag. I flip to the next letter, and then I turn to him.

"Do you really want these? Or are you just reading them for me?" I ask. He thinks for a minute.

"Both, I guess," he says. "I know it's helpful to you, but I also like the little glimpses into the pieces of your life I missed. For a minute, it's like I was there."

I nod then reluctantly hand over the next letter.

RYDER,

WE JUST GOT BACK from the doctor. It's official: I miscarried.

I FELT off when I woke up the other day. It was weird. And then the bleeding started.

TWELVE WEEKS. The doctor said I'm pretty far along to have miscarried. Most women miscarry earlier on. Lucky me.

I MISS the way you could make me smile when it felt like the world was caving in.

. . .

BUT THEN YOU caved in my world.

Mila

HE READS the letter again then folds it up and sticks it in his pocket. Then he takes one, two, three steps toward me, and before I can react, his arms are around me. He pulls me into him, enveloping me in his grasp, my cheek against his hard chest. I feel his lips press gently down against the top of my head, and I feel my knees buckle beneath me.

My God, it feels good to be in his arms again.

Too good.

I let him hold me for a moment before the scent, the memory, and the desire to stay like this for the rest of the night becomes too much. He can feel me pulling away before I actually do it, and slowly, he lets his arms fall.

"You would have made an amazing mother, Mila," he whispers, letting his hand rest gently under my chin for a moment. My eyes drop to the ground, and I turn back to my car. But before I do, I call out his name.

"I want to go to your appointment with you next week," I tell him. His eyes narrow in on me, then he nods and smiles.

"It's a date."

14

THEN, SUMMER BEFORE JUNIOR YEAR

"Mila, hurry up!" Chase calls up the stairs. I'm ignoring him while I scrunch some mousse in my hair and tousle my waves, making sure they bounce just right. There's a bonfire tonight, somewhere up on the mountain, with the group we've been hanging with all summer long. I check the time on my phone and see the date, and it makes my stomach flip.

One week. I have one more week with him.

In just seven weeks, Ryder Casey has taken what I thought life was all about and flipped it on its end. I've spent my whole life quiet. I've spent it reserved, in the background of most scenarios I've found myself in. But with him, I'm loud. With him, I can say it all without actually having to say a word.

But in seven days, I go back home. And he stays here, in this magical place, without me.

I trot down the steps with a little more pep in my step, suddenly hyperaware of every minute that passes.

Chase is out the door ahead of me, and Mom and Dad are calling their goodbyes from the kitchen.

But as I step out onto the front porch, I freeze when I see him, perched on the hood of his truck, waiting for me. Chase gives him a quick nod. They've become much more civil, which is good for me.

I don't *need* Chase to be my protector. I don't need him to vet the guys—or guy, I should say—that I'm interested in. But I do need my brother. I need him to be the rock he's always been, the constant in my life that's never faltering.

"I could have brought her, man," he tells Ryder, but Ryder smiles and shakes his head.

"I know," he says, "but I wanted to bring my date."

He looks up at me and smiles just as Chase chuckles and hops in his own truck.

"You two are a little nauseating." He smiles out the window before speeding away.

"You didn't have to do this," I say, stepping off the front porch. He smiles and shrugs.

"I figured it would be pretty awkward to kiss you tonight in front of your brother or anyone else that's at this thing," he says. My eyes widen into big saucers as I stare up at him.

"What?"

He shrugs again.

"If it's alright with you, I'm planning on kissing you tonight," he says. I clear my throat as my cheeks flush with fire. "Sorry it's taken me all summer. I guess I just wanted to make sure it was perfect. There's a lot riding on it."

He steps closer to me, looping his arms around my waist.

It's been seven weeks, and he's not so much as pecked me on the cheek.

"There is?" I ask. He nods, stepping closer and intertwining our fingers.

"I don't know if I'll be your last first kiss," he says, "but I want you to remember it for the rest of your life."

Then, he pulls away and opens my door, letting me hop in. I smile to myself as I try not to let the combined fear and excitement show on my face.

I've been kissed exactly two times in my whole life.

Once was on a dare in eighth grade. James Bird. It lasted all of 0.43 seconds, and I barely got my eyes closed before it was over.

The second was last year, after school. Tommy Roberts. Outside of the gym. He'd talked to me all summer long, texting me relentlessly, casually dropping by to visit with my brother. He had me pushed up against the brick wall of the school, and when he dropped his head to mine, I could smell the sweat on him from football practice.

He leaned in, and as our lips touched, I remember feeling a wave of disappointment. It wasn't this life-halting, time-stopping moment I'd been waiting for, pining after all summer long. And when he slowly slid his hand up my hip and tried to dip it under my shirt, I swatted it away.

And when he gave me a weird look and slowly tried it again, I swatted him harder.

And then my brother turned the corner.

And you can guess how that went.

Chase had in-school suspension for three days once Principal Lorrence saw Tommy's shiner.

I needed my brother to protect me then.

But with Ryder, I don't feel that. I *want* Chase around, but I don't need him to protect me from having my heart broken or my innocence taken away. I think it's because, after just seven short weeks, I feel like Ryder wants to protect all those things just as badly as Chase does.

Ryder drives up the road a bit, crossing over a little bridge and turning left onto some of the backroads that we've been driving around all summer. When we get to Stone Brook Park, he parks and does a little jog around to my side then opens the door and gently lifts me out.

He takes my hand and leads me down a path to the firepit where our summer crew has been meeting up every week since I met them. It's funny that I've been in Kelford with the same people my entire life, yet I feel more at home here in Meade Lake with these people than I ever have at home.

"'Bout time," Derrick says, shooting us a look and a smile. I blush as Ryder pushes a log big enough for both of us up closer to the fire.

"They just *had* to ride alone," Chase says, laughing with Derrick and leaning back on his own log.

Luna and Daniel are nestled in a chair, barely aware of anyone else in the world.

Derrick's brother, Teddy, is also sitting next to him, poking at the fire with a big stick.

"Did anyone bring booze?" Kirby asks, shuffling down the path with Jules in tow. Kirby is short and stout with bouncing black curls and an attitude that you can feel for miles. But she's funny, and so far this summer, I've remained on her good side—something I prefer to keep doing.

Jules is her cousin; they're a year apart. Jules is tall

with auburn hair and deep, brown eyes. She usually comes as a set of three with her friends Shane and Mikey, but they're both working at the arcade tonight.

This group is something I've never experienced before; they are all close; there's no cattiness; there's no gossip among them. They are quick to call one another out, but they're quick to laugh, too. It's like they match their surroundings. They're loud and boisterous like the water in the wakes, but they stand up tall like the mountains around them, creating a boundary around each other. A boundary I think I have around me now. They've all grown up here in Meade Lake, a vacation town, watching people come and go on a daily basis, trying to escape the tourism they were bred into.

"I believe it was Teddy's night," Jules says, sitting down next to Luna and Daniel.

"Shit…" Teddy mutters.

"Aww, Jesus Christ, Ted. This is the one fucking night a week I get to do something other than take tickets at the fucking movie theater. You had *one* job," Kirby says, throwing her hands up in the air as she crashes down onto another chair.

"Sorry, Kirb," he mutters. Derrick playfully punches him in the arm as we all laugh.

"So, you two are outta here soon, huh?" Jules asks, reaching forward to grab a chip from the bag on Daniel's knee.

Chase and I look at each other. I feel Ryder's arm slide up around my body, tugging me closer to him lightly.

"Yeah," Chase says. "Next week."

"Damn," Kirby says. "I almost forgot you two weren't locals."

"Me, too," Derrick says with a nod. Ryder's grip tightens around me, and I swallow.

"So, what's the plan with you two?" Kirby asks, pointing from Ryder to me. My eyes widen, and I turn to Ryder slowly. God, please let him answer so I don't have to.

"What about us?" he asks. *Ah, good. Deflection.*

"Don't '*what about us*' me," Kirby says with a smirk. Derrick chuckles from behind her. "I mean, what's the deal? You together, not together? Staying together if you are?"

I feel the heat rising on my cheeks, and my palms start to get clammy in my pockets. There's an awkward silence, then Chase clears his throat and jumps to his feet.

"How cold does this water get at night?" he asks. Everyone turns to him, including me, and I want to hug him. I know what he's doing. Saving me. Again.

"Huh?"

"Anyone up for a skinny dip?" he asks. I look around as everyone's eyebrows shoot up. Chase strips his shirt off over his head and lets it drop in a ball at his feet. My brother is ripped, and judging by the looks on almost all of the female faces around me, he's not hard to look at. He tugs his jeans down and sprints toward the dock in front of us in nothing but his boxers.

Suddenly, the rest of the group is on their feet, and clothes start flying. Thankfully, no one goes full nude, but some of the undergarments leave little to the imagination. Then, like a herd of wild animals in heat, they take off down the shore, onto the dock, and into the black water.

I look up at Ryder. He knows I won't go. He knows I

won't take my clothes off or join the group. He smiles and takes my hand in his again.

"Wanna go for a walk?" he asks. I wonder if I wasn't here, if he would be in the water with them. *Am I holding him back?* His eyes trail out to them, swimming, splashing, screeching. He smiles then looks down at me. "I just want to be wherever you are."

My heart thuds against my chest. So much of what I've felt, been uncomfortable with, worried about over the last few weeks, Ryder has anticipated. He's acted on it, finding ways to make me feel comfortable, finding ways to avoid situations that might not be the most natural for me. Just like Chase has always done for me.

I've lived with anxiety my whole life. It's not really a secret in our house. Everyone knows it. But my parents have sort of ignored it. Chase, though…he's always been the one. He's always been the one to protect me from my own illness, my own weakness.

And in just two months, Ryder has picked up on it and doesn't make me feel weird about it. When I don't grab for a drink—when Teddy remembers to bring booze, that is—for fear of being caught, Ryder doesn't even look that way. He doesn't ask if I want to join certain scenarios—like jumping half-naked off a dock, for example—because he can feel I don't want to.

There's something about it, something about the way he can feel the move I'm going to make before I do, that has my whole world trembling.

"Sure," I say, squeezing his hand and pulling him closer to me. It's still summer, but it gets cooler here at night. I "accidentally" forgot a coat again, and it has nothing to do with the fact that Ryder always has one and *always* lends it to me.

"So," I say as we follow the path farther into the woods. A slow smile tugs at one corner of his lips.

"So," he says, "guess we have some questions to answer."

I nod as he turns to me. The water peeks through the trees at the edge of the woods behind us, and the moon lights up the earth like it's trying to compensate for the deep mountain darkness.

I look up at him. He tucks a stray strand of hair behind my ear.

"Why does it feel like I've known you longer than just a summer?" I ask him. He chuckles.

"Another life, I guess." He shrugs. I smile and look down at the ground. He cups my face in his hands and lets his thumbs graze my cheeks.

"I hope I know you in all my lives," I whisper. He smiles down at me again, and then before I can prepare, he leans down and lets his lips land gently on mine. I reach up and grasp onto his wrists, letting him lead the way. He grips onto me tighter, wrapping one arm around my waist now. His thumb still strokes my cheek, and his fingers wrap gently into my hair. I don't hear the lapping of the water against the docks. I don't feel the cool mountain breeze that normally leaves chills across my skin. I don't feel the weight of the unknown that I've been anxious about for the last few weeks. I don't feel anything but him, right now, in this moment.

We stand there, entwined in what I'm pretty sure is going to be an unbeatable kiss, before he slowly pulls back. He looks down at me and raises an eyebrow. I smile and press my lips together like I'm trying to stamp his kiss on me forever.

"So…? How was that?" he asks. I laugh.

"I won't be forgetting that one anytime soon," I say. He leans down and kisses me again, this time wrapping both arms around me and lifting my feet off the ground. When he lowers me gently, everything comes back down to Earth with me, including the uncertainty that I've been keeping at bay.

He leans down and presses his forehead to mine, and it's almost like he's trying to take it away, trying to absorb it for me.

"Mila?" he asks.

"Hmm?" I ask without taking my head from his.

"I really don't care where you are. I just want you," he says. I pull back and look up at him.

"I want you, too," I say, swallowing back the lump that's forming in my throat.

"Kelford is only two hours away, right?" he asks. I nod. "Piece of cake."

I nod again, forcing a smile. He nudges me.

"Hey," he says. I make myself look up at him, and those big blue eyes take my breath away again, just like they've done all summer. "This is just our beginning."

I smile and wrap my arms around his neck, burying my face into him.

15

"Earth to Mila," Derrick says with a whistle, waving a hand in my face as I stare off the dock and into the water.

"Oh, sorry," I say, jumping to attention. "Did you need me?" It's been a busy day on the water today. We've been completely sold out since ten this morning, on everything from pontoons to kayaks. I'm just sitting on the dock, waiting for the last straggling renters to make their way back in. It's just Derrick and me today, though. It's Ryder's day off, and he's home with Annabelle.

"Nah," he says, shaking his head and sitting down next to me on the dock. "Things are dying down 'cause it's starting to get dark."

I nod and lean back against the shed. I feel him next to me as we both look off in silence, both with the same weight laying heavy on our minds.

"So, he told you the rest?" he asks. I look at him and nod. "I told ya. He's been through a lot."

I nod again.

"How bad was it the first time?" I ask.

Derrick lets out a sigh and lets his head rest back against the shed.

"Well, it was bad enough that I had to go with him to have his will written up," he says, and my breath catches in my throat. All these times, all these years, I've cursed Ryder's name, his very existence. Wished he were dead instead of my brother.

But hearing about the will he had drafted suddenly makes all those wishes feel heavy around me. And it makes me sick.

"But then the treatment finally started to work, and within just a few weeks, the tumor was almost completely gone," he goes on. His big brown eyes look out across the water. "I always thought it was such bull-shit, the way he had to go through all that and then lose her so soon after."

My eyes drop.

"You know what he told me after Maura passed?" he asks. I look over to him. "We scattered her ashes up on the mountain, and when the urn was empty, he put it down and looked at me. Told me it was karma. He told me all of it, everything, was because of what he'd done."

My eyes are wide, and I can feel my breath quickening. I wrap my arms around myself and stare out over the water.

"What...what did you say?" I whisper.

Derrick pushes off the dock as we see three red kayaks in the distance headed for us. He turns back to me.

"I told him I didn't believe in karma, and like every other storm, we'd get through it. We just had a pretty angel looking over us for the rest of our journey," Derrick says. A sad smile flutters across my lips as my eyes slowly look to the clouds. I wonder about Maura, who she was, what she was like. How she loved Ryder. I've thought about her a lot since I learned about her. Wondering if she loved him the way I did. Not in terms of competition, just in terms of *how*. Did she feel like the ground beneath her shifted when he was around? Like bridges were built to help her navigate the rest of her life just because he was in it?

Probably. Loving Ryder was magical that way.

I help Derrick collect the last of the life vests and drag the kayaks up the hill and across the street to the shop. We rack them at the back of the store, put away the last of the forms, and start to close everything up and turn everything off. He holds the door for me at the front of the store as I pull my hair out from under my sweat jacket.

"Derrick?" I ask him just before he ducks into his truck.

"Hmm?"

"Do you really not believe in karma?" I ask.

A smile creeps across his lips, and he flashes those perfect teeth.

"Ya know, I really, truly didn't," he says. "Thought it was all a bunch of bull. But I guess I kind of do now."

"Why now?" I ask.

"Because you showed back up right when he needed you around. That has to be good karma," he says with a shrug. "And if ever there was someone who deserved some good karma, it's Ryder Casey." Then, he throws his truck in reverse and speeds off.

. . .

I TURN onto Joan's Way and head toward our house when I see him perched on the porch, fiddling with his keys. He pops up when he hears my tires over the gravel.

"Ryder?" I say as I get out. "What are you doing here?"

He doesn't answer; he just smiles and walks toward me. I freeze. That smile still does things to me.

"Do you wanna meet my kid?" he asks, stopping mere inches in front of me. I swallow.

"Wha...what? I thought you—"

"Yeah, I did," he says with a shrug, "but I figure if you're voluntarily coming with me to hear my fate tomorrow, the least I could do is introduce you." He chuckles but freezes immediately when he sees the look on my face.

"Hey," he says, nudging me. "I'm fine, okay? I have to say, though, it's nice to know you're worried about me."

He flashes this devilish smile, one I haven't seen in over a decade, and for the first time since I've been back in Meade Lake, I'm...ahem...awakened.

"Who says I'm worried?" I ask, sticking out a hip and crossing my arms over my chest. He smiles again.

"I may have missed a lot, but I still know you, Mila," he says. I bite my lip to keep from smiling, and I feel the heat on my cheeks.

"Well, *anyway,*" I say, "I would love to meet her."

"Great," he says with that grin. "How's tomorrow sound? After the appointment?"

I smile and nod.

"That sounds great. I'll pick you up tomorrow around three, we can go get the results, and then head home and have an early dinner. I promised her she could swim, so bring a bathing suit."

My eyes give me away.

"It's okay if you don't have one; we sell them at the store. You can grab one tomorrow morning, if you want."

I smile and nod. It's not the fact that I didn't bring one; it's the idea of being in front of Ryder in nothing but a bathing suit after all these years.

It's the idea of seeing *him* in a bathing suit after all these years. Because if there's one thing that doesn't seem to have changed, it's his physique. He somehow seems even *more* youthful than he did in his, well, youth.

His t-shirts always cling to his muscles. They bulge out of his arms when he lifts the kayaks from the water. And that quick little glimpse I got in the shed that day I fell in...*whoo*. I might need to bring a fan with me tomorrow.

Shit.

THE NEXT MORNING, I'm up with the sun in this huge-ass lake house all by myself. I wonder if my dad is missing the rental income he's currently not making off this house because of his almost-thirty-year-old daughter who is currently squatting in it. But one thing at a time.

That thing is supposed to be forgiving Ryder. Figuring out why I'm such a shitshow. Figuring out why, since my brother left me, I'm destined to fuck up anything and everything in my life.

But the longer I'm here, the harder it's getting to remember how or why I could ever hate Ryder so much to begin with. And that's fucking terrifying.

I make a cup of coffee and sit out on the back deck, lounging on one of the huge chaises that points out toward the water. We were really lucky little shits, growing up coming here all those years. Having it all to ourselves when they would leave us.

Looking back on it now, though, that was when Chase and I were the happiest. When we were away from my parents.

It's a hard thing to put into words, the resentment I feel toward them. I guess because of the financial aspect —we had everything we could ever need, and then some, so who were we to complain?

But it didn't change the fact that Chase and I relied on each other for that connection that we were missing from them. And as I got older, I realized we were missing it from them because they were missing it from each other.

When I discovered the affair that year I met Ryder, it felt like my world was crumbling. My parents bickered a lot, Mom being dragged to all the parties with him, plastering on the perfect-wife smile. It wasn't a secret that they weren't happy. But knowing that there was so *much* wrong with their marriage that he had to find what he was looking for somewhere else was devastating.

But the worst of it was the silence.

That, still to this day, neither of them have uttered a word to me about it. It's as if it didn't happen. They're still unhappy, but they coexist well.

The ultimate betrayal wasn't that my dad cheated. It was that he cheated, she found out about it, and then left us in the dark.

When I met Ryder, that was when my world was opened up to the possibilities of a functional relationship. Of actually being happy with the person you were with...what a freakin' concept.

But then everything happened, and it just reaffirmed what I had grown to know. Nothing lasts, except for the bad.

Even if, at one point in time, that something felt so, *so* good.

AFTER A LITTLE WHILE longer on the deck, I remember that I have a swimming date tomorrow and no bathing suit. I hop in my car and head up into town toward the shop. I see Derrick out by the boats, and I smile because that means that someone *else* is probably inside. I park my car and hop out, ready to see his smiling face at the counter. But as I'm passing the door to the coffee shop, I freeze when I come mere inches from a big, heaving chest covered in dark navy. A badge glistens in the sun, and I read the name on his lapel: M. Trout.

I freeze, my whole body locking up.

"Oh, excuse me, ma'am," he says with a warm smile. He slides to the side of the walkway to let me through, and at first, I don't think he remembers me.

But then he does a double take.

"Do I...do I know you?" he asks, his eyebrows knit together and his head cocked to one side. I swallow what feels like knives.

I can see the red and blue flashing lights; I can hear the sirens.

I can hear Officer Trout shouting for backup as he pumps my brother's chest.

And then I can feel his hands on me, his arms

around me, carrying me away from the scene when he realizes it's all over.

"I...uh, my name is—" I start to say and pause to clear my throat, trying to find the right words. *You tried, and failed, to save my brother's life twelve years ago.* "I don't think so," I finally say. "I'm from out of town. Just visiting."

He tilts his head back some, purses his lips, then nods his head.

"Well, welcome to Meade Lake. Hope you enjoy your stay," he says with a tip of an imaginary hat as he walks away.

I look up, and my eyes meet Ryder's from across the lot.

I know he's thinking what I'm thinking. I know he's flooded with the memories. I know his feelings mirror mine.

And I can't take it.

I take in a deep breath and turn back to my car, driving off to the house. He doesn't call after me; he doesn't follow. He knows.

Whatever is happening here, whatever shit we're stirring up from the past, it can't undo what happened. As hard as it's getting to remember, it's a dangerous game I'm playing.

I cannot fall back in love with him. Because as Officer Trout just reminded me, history cannot be rewritten.

I'M SITTING on the back deck again with that same book, flipping through the pages idly when I hear tires over the gravel out front. I hop up from the chaise and start to head inside, but I hear footsteps coming from around the side of the house.

"Hey," he says, a sheepish, worried look in his eye as he stuffs his hands into his jean pockets.

"Hey," I say, turning toward him and wrapping my arms around myself.

"I wasn't sure if you still wanted to, uh, to come today," he says, jutting a thumb toward his truck. I swallow. With the blast from the past at the shop, I almost forgot that I was supposed to be spending the day with him. Meet his daughter.

"I, uh…" I start. His eyes drop to the ground.

"I'm sorry, Mila," he says. I stare at him. "I know you remembered Trout from the night of the accident."

I stare, trying to even out my breathing. He goes on.

"I know it has to be hard being here in general. I know you probably see him everywhere."

I just keep staring.

"But for the record, I'm so glad you came back."

I let out the breath I didn't know I was holding.

"Even if you never forgive me, even if you can't get past it all…seeing you again has been…I don't know. I can't explain it. Just good for my soul, I guess."

There's a long, awkward pause as my insides fight over how to respond. My brain is trying to formulate the right words, the words that won't hurt Ryder but also won't betray the memory of my dead brother.

But like he always did, he knows I need him to keep talking.

"I totally get it if you need some space. But just know that whenever you want, for as long as you want, you're always welcome here."

His eyes are fixed on mine, like they're drilling holes

straight into me. Then he smiles a sad smile and turns to walk off the deck.

"Ryder," I call out to him. He stops and turns back. "I just need to grab my bag."

I turn on my heel and head in through the back door. And if I'm not mistaken, there's a hint of a smile on his face.

16

W e're riding down Lake Shore Highway toward Timberland, the next town over, where Ryder's oncologist has an office. It's been a relatively quiet ride; Ryder has the windows down and the radio turned up, but we haven't really spoken. I have my hand out the window, letting the wind blow through my fingers.

"I didn't think you were gonna come," he finally says. I turn to him and tuck my feet up on the seat.

"I told you I wanted to," I say.

"I know. But that was before you ran into Trout. And I just—"

"Hey," I say, cutting him off and placing my hand on top of his for the briefest of moments. "I want to go with you."

He smiles and nods. After a few more minutes of silence, he lets out a soft chuckle as he reaches a hand out his own window.

"What?" I ask him.

"Nothin'," he says with a smile.

"Hey, that's not fair. Tell me," I say, and I can't help but smile back at him.

"I said your name when I came to," he says. My eyes widen, and I turn my whole body to face him.

"What? When?" I ask. "When you came to when?"

"When I had the seizure, the first time—when I had cancer," he says, clearing his throat. I cringe at the words "first time." Because it means he's thinking that there could be a second time.

"You...you said my name? But weren't you with—"

"My wife, yeah," he says with a chuckle, but I'm failing to see what's funny about it. "When I opened my eyes, and the black specks finally faded away, my head was in her lap. I was staring up at the sky, and she said I just kept repeating your name. She didn't tell me till I was in remission."

I nod slowly, so, so confused.

"Was she...mad?"

He shakes his head and leans his head back against the headrest.

"Nope. Not my Maura," he smiles. "It took a lot to get her mad. I apologized profusely, but she told me not to be sorry. She said she believed that when we were in our most vulnerable states, we thought about unfinished business. And she always said you were mine."

His eyes are trained on the road ahead of him, and his lips break out into a smile again.

"What? What are you smiling about?"

"I don't know. I guess just the fact that you're here...I don't know," he says. I turn back to face the road and pull my feet up onto the seat underneath me.

After a few more minutes, we finally pull into the picturesque mountain town of Timberland, tucked away on the Pennsylvania border. It looks like one of the towns you see on Christmas cards: churches with big steeples and tiny, old houses peeking out of the mountainside. We pull off the highway, make a few turns, and park in front of a big brick building.

A big black sign reads "R.H. Oncology Associates" in gold letters ahead of us. Before I unbuckle my seatbelt, he's at my door, opening it for me just like he used to do. I swallow as we get out.

"You ready?" he asks me. I can't help but smile.

"Are *you*?" I ask him. He shrugs and smiles back.

I follow him inside and take a seat on one of the bright-yellow waiting room chairs while he checks in.

"Mr. Casey, it's been a long while since we've seen your smilin' face up here!" a plump woman with bleach-blonde hair calls out from behind the desk.

"Hey, Claudia," he says with that killer smile. "You weren't here the other day when I was in. Before that, it's been a few years. How have you been?"

She comes around the desk and wraps her arms around him.

"We've been real good," she says. "How's that sweet baby of yours?"

"She's great," he says. "Growing more every day, I swear."

I get that warm feeling in my belly again, anytime he talks about her. There's this look in his eye, and I know he never, will never, look at anyone or anything the way he must look at her.

"They do that," Claudia says with a wink. Then her eyes catch me, and I clear my throat awkwardly.

"This is my...this is Mila. We've known each other

for years," he says. "She's here today for moral support. Even though I *know* we're in the clear, right?"

Claudia smiles and cocks her head, giving him a look that says *don't get ahead of yourself.*

"Good mojo, ladies!" Ryder says.

"Good mojo," Claudia repeats in unison with another woman from behind the desk.

"Come on back, y'all," Claudia says, waving us back down a long hall. We pass a few exam rooms then stop in front of a door. She taps on it and pushes it open.

"Mr. Casey's ready for you," Claudia tells the man behind the door. A tall, slender man in a white coat stands up to greet us. He's older, maybe mid-sixties, and is at least two inches taller than Ryder.

"Mr. Casey, come on in," he says, holding a hand out. Claudia closes the door behind us, and the doctor points to the two chairs on the other side of his desk.

"How are we today?" he asks, smoothing out his coat and sitting down. He folds his long hands on the desk in front of him, looking from me, to Ryder, to me, to Ryder.

"Good, doc, doin' real good," Ryder says. "This is an old friend, Mila. She's here for moral support." He smiles that smile, and so far, I've never met anyone who can't *not* smile back.

"Hello, Mila," the doctor says, nodding in my direction. "I'm Dr. Chandler."

"Hi," I say. "Nice to meet you."

"Likewise. Shall we?" he asks, holding up a file folder. Ryder pauses and holds his hands up.

"Hang on there, doc," he says, leaning back in the chair. He stretches his legs out and shakes out his arms, making himself comfortable. "Okay. I'm ready," he says.

I can still sense things on another level with Ryder, like I used to.

His lips are smiling, but his eyes aren't.

He's scared.

And that makes me scared. I clear my throat and lean forward.

"Well, Ryder," Dr. Chandler says, pulling some scans from the folder, "as you know, we found a mass on your last scans."

My eyes move to Ryder. He said "abnormal." He didn't mention any mass.

"So the biopsy results are back," Dr. Chandler continues. Then he pauses and stretches an arm across the desk. He wraps his fingers around Ryder's arm. "Son, the cancer is back."

17

We've been driving in silence for about twenty minutes. I don't know what to say, but then, in situations like this, does anyone, really? When someone's world is flipped on its axis, when you can practically hear the crash of all that they knew coming to a dead stop, does anyone actually know what to say?

Words feel wasted right now. I have no answers. I don't know what he's thinking. There was a time when I knew what was going through his mind without even having to look at him. But too much time has passed. We have some catching up to do, I guess.

Is there still time?

We finally drive over a mountain, and I see Meade Bridge in the distance. We're almost there. Almost home.

Home.

But when we cross the bridge, he makes a right turn instead of a left toward town and both of our houses.

And I know where he's going. We went there a few times.

His truck rumbles as he drives up the steep mountain road. His eyes stare straight out the windshield, but I know he's not really seeing anything. We pull off onto the side road once we reach the top, and the pavement turns to dust as he rumbles through. We drive straight down the road, and I take a look around. Back in the day, the whole top of this mountain was untouched, unclaimed, uninhabited. Now, huge houses peek out of all sides, the chair lift sliding down between them, taking the skiers to their destination during the winter months. I can see the huge lodge in the distance, and my heart is almost sad at how much this place has changed.

Now, it looks like the only part of this mountain that hasn't been touched is this half, with only this dirt road cutting through the unkempt grass. He drives a little bit farther, until we reach a clearing in the trees, and puts the truck in park. He hops out and walks a little ahead of me toward the edge of the mountain. All that's around now is him, me, the trees, and the view of the lake below. *Our lake.*

I stand back by the truck, trying to give him some space. I watch as he walks across the open field, his thick arms swaying in fury, his hands balled into fists. His heather-red t-shirt is tight across his back muscles, and even in this state, he's pretty beautiful.

But seeing him like this is a little unsettling. Ever since I got back to Meade Lake—well, actually, ever since I've known him—he's been gentle. He's a jokester; he's mischievous; he's wild. But he's also soft, and gentle, and thoughtful. He's the one that waited for me to be comfortable enough to tell my parents about us.

He's the one who never brought up going all the way when we were kids until I did.

He's the one.

He was the one.

He gets as close to the edge of the mountain top as possible, and my stomach does a flip. Then, he lets out a long, pained scream that hits me at my core and steals the breath from my lungs. When it's over, he crouches down on the ground, letting his head fall in his hands.

And in this moment, I can feel my own world starting to flip on its axis.

Because in this moment, I realize that I can't hate him. I don't hate him. And I also realize that I still love him. I'm drowning in a mix of crazy emotions, fear of this revelation, but also pure, unadulterated joy in this revelation. And the truest terror I've ever felt about the fact that, in a few months from now, it might not matter anyway.

"I don't like to put a number on these things, Ryder, you know that," Dr. Chandler had told him earlier. Ryder gave him a look.

"Doc, please," he had said. "I have a little girl now. What are my chances if the treatment doesn't work? How long?"

I had held my breath while Dr. Chandler hesitated.

"I truly don't know, Ryder. It depends on how aggressive this is. But judging by its size, I guess about six months."

I had felt like I was going to faint.

I suck in a long, slow breath then make my way toward him. I slowly kneel down in the grass next to him. I see his shoulders trembling, and I can feel a crack in the hardass foundation I've been working so hard at keeping up these last few weeks.

I reach a hand out and put it on his shoulder, then the other. I pull him toward me, and he lets his head drop to my shoulder. I wrap my arms around him tight, and I feel him wrap his around my waist. And I don't even know how much time passes.

But we just sit there, me holding him, him letting out what he can't let out in front of Annabelle. Or maybe, in front of anyone else.

I've only seen him like this one other time. When his mom left.

Finally, he takes in a long breath and pulls back gently. He plops down on the ground and looks out over the sprawling landscape ahead of us. The sky is streaked with pinks and oranges, a sure sign that the sun is on its way out for the night. The trees on the mountains in the distance are turning black as the sunlight slowly fades away into the thick clouds above us.

"I didn't see this coming," he finally says.

I drop back next to him, and my eyes find his. I let him go on.

"I have no idea…" he starts to say, but his voice trails off. He grabs a pebble from the ground next to him and chucks it off the mountain. I reach back and let my arm cross over his, scooting closer to him.

"Hey," I say, imploring him to look at me. He does. "You don't have to have all the answers right now."

He scoffs.

"I don't have *any* answers right now," he says.

"That's not true," I tell him. "You know you're starting treatment next week. You know you have six months of chemo, and you know that Dr. Chandler thinks you have a good prognosis."

Positive. Keep with the positive.

He snorts.

"I don't even know what I'm going to do with Annabelle for all that," he says hopelessly. "Alma is already watching her four days a week. I don't know how I can fit treatment in the midst of two jobs and trying to keep up with the shop and everything. I didn't have Annabelle last time. And I *did* have Maura."

I swallow.

"I know," I say, squeezing his hand. "But you *do* have Annabelle. And you have me."

He lifts his eyes to me, his brows raised high. I interlace my fingers with his.

"I'm not leaving until your last treatment. I'll work extra hours at the shop, and Derrick can show me how to do inventory. And I'll work it out with him so that I can be with Annabelle when Alma can't. We got this," I tell him. He squeezes my hand back. Slowly, he pulls himself up and reaches down to me to pull me to my feet. He wraps his hands around my waist, and my pulse quickens. He pulls me in close to him and bends his head down to rest his on mine.

"This isn't why you came," he says. "This isn't fair to you. You came here so you could move on with your life. Not stop everything in its tracks for me."

I take a step closer and let my fingers link around his back.

"Maybe stopping here *is* moving on with my life," I say. I open my eyes and see a little smile tug on the corner of his lips. It does my heart good that, in a moment as bleak as this, I can still bring some brightness to him.

He sighs and tightens his grip. Then we come apart, and he turns back to the mountains.

"How am I supposed to leave her?" he whispers. His words hit me like a wave, rattling me around until I find earth again beneath me.

I know he's not asking me. And it's a good thing, because I don't have the answer.

18

THEN, JUNIOR YEAR

"Mila, come on!" Chase calls up the stairs. "We're waiting for you. You're gonna make us late!"

I'm sitting in front of the mirror at my vanity, just staring. I'm in the gorgeous dress my mom bought for me. It's a swirl of purples and blues and has this elegant open back. It makes me feel sexy without feeling like I have to show too much skin. I'm not comfortable with it like some of the other girls in our class—like Chase's date will be tonight.

It's the Winter Wonderland dance at school, but I'm not looking forward to it. Chase is going with Marley Shepard, who is fine, I guess. She's on the pom squad, and she's also the student council secretary. She's nice to me, but we just run in different crowds.

Well, sort of. I don't really have a crowd. Chase is my crowd.

Chase and the kids from Meade Lake. But that's just it. They're in Meade Lake.

I look over at the only framed photo on my vanity.

It's Ryder and me wrapped around each other at the edge of the lake. Luna took it at the last bonfire we had before we left this past summer.

I was looking forward to the dance this year because I actually had a date. *My* date. My Ryder.

But now, he can't come. My parents are disappointed. Chase asked if he broke up with me, and when I told him no, he seemed to drop it. He's quick to be on the defensive, if necessary. But since it was a non-brother emergency, he quickly turned his attention back to gelling his hair and spraying on copious amounts of cologne.

I sigh and then start the trek down the stairs. Chase is waiting at the bottom, jiggling his keys in his hand. I'll have to squeeze in the back of his truck in my dress and sit in the back like a child while he picks up his date. I'll stand at the edge of the group photos awkwardly. I'll probably end up alone most of the night, anyway—which is normally how I prefer it.

Until I met Ryder. He makes me not want to be alone.

I get to the bottom, and I look around. I look from Mom, to Dad, to Chase.

"I don't think I'm gonna go," I tell them. Chase cocks an eyebrow at me.

"What do you mean?" Dad asks. "What...just because that boy can't go?"

I roll my eyes. "That boy" has been Dad's name for Ryder since he officially introduced himself toward the end of the summer.

Dad seemed less than pleased that my summer fling proved to be a little bit more than that. Particularly because he's not from Kelford, he's not the son of a doctor in town, and he's not into politics.

Mom doesn't really have an opinion. She doesn't bring him up a lot; it's almost like she doesn't want to discuss men at all.

"I think I want to go visit Ryder," I say.

Chase's eyes are wide as he looks to my parents then back to me, waiting for a response.

"I think you should. That's where you wanna be anyway," he finally says. I smile at him.

"That's silly. You're all dressed up already. What'll people think if you don't show up now?"

As badly as my dad wants me to be *somebody*, moments like these kill him, I know.

"Dad, not a single soul will miss me," I tell him.

"That's not true," Chase says. "I will. But I want you to have a good time, too."

I smile at him again.

"Come on, now. You don't need to miss this dance. You'll have a good time. What about that Cindy girl? You were friends with her," Dad says.

I scoff.

"Dad, Cindy Harper was my friend in third grade," I tell him. He rolls his eyes.

"Well, regardless, you should go to the dance. It's just silly to miss," he says. I swallow. I should have known he'd object to me missing some sort of social event. God forbid I miss an opportunity to spread the good word of John Walton.

"You should go to Meade Lake," Mom says from across the foyer. She has her arms crossed over her chest. Dad whips his head around to her.

"Carla, that's silly. You went and got her all dressed up, and—"

"Is his mother home?" Mom cuts him off. I turn to her.

"No, but he's staying with his aunt," I lie—something I've rarely done in my lifetime, which is why they never question me. She thinks for a moment then smiles.

"You should go, honey. Go ahead and get out of that thing. We can probably still return it."

She walks toward me and kisses my cheek. I throw my arms around her neck and run up the stairs.

It's sick, because I know part of the reason she is pushing me is because it's the opposite of what my dad wants. Ever since his affair, the resentment in the house is thick. My mom is spiteful, bitter. She pushes back on my dad on just about everything. And he never says a word when she does.

Chase is still oblivious to it all. But me, I take advantage of it. If they're not going to be straight with me, then I'll milk it for all it's worth.

I tear my dress off and throw on a sweatshirt and some jeans, and I'm back down the steps before Chase has even left.

He calls out to me before we get in our cars.

"Be careful," he tells me. "And tell Ryder I said hey."

I smile and nod.

That's my brother's way of saying, "I care about you. And I approve of him." And both mean more to me than anyone knows.

I'm not telling him I'm coming because I know he won't want me to come take care of him. He has some nasty bug, and I know he's all alone. His mom is out of town—again—and Aunt Winnie is somewhere across the sea on one of her grand trips she's always taking.

Ryder and I have officially been together for about five months now, but it feels longer than that. It feels like my whole life I've been wearing this mask, and I only just took it off when he became mine.

We've visited each other as much as we can. Weekends are hard with his shifts at the diner, but we've made it work. Usually, when his mom isn't home, Aunt Winnie takes him in. I've met his mom only twice, and she seemed totally unaware of the fact that she had a teenage son both times. Uninterested, disengaged. She had Ryder at seventeen, and from what I gather, instead of quickly rushing to mature for the sake of her son, she froze in time and is now living out the years that she felt were stolen from her.

He doesn't know his dad, aside from the measly check he sends every month to his mother. He was the football star at Meade Lake High School, and his parents refused to let a "setback" such as a child ruin that future for him. They offered Ryder's grandmother a big chunk of money when he was born, and his father pays child support monthly still. But most of the money is gone, and he says he knows his father is waiting for the day he turns eighteen to cut him off completely. He's married and lives in Maine with his two lovely daughters, whom Ryder has never met.

But Aunt Winnie, she's special.

She's his mom's younger sister, but she takes care of Ryder. There's this gleam in her eyes when she looks at him that his mother doesn't have. Like she'd try and stop the world from turning for him. She also *politely* told me that she'd kick my ass if I hurt him. I like her.

Now that Chase is in the thick of basketball season, I'm even more thankful for Ryder. He's been the escape I didn't know I needed. Well, he's the escape that I never *did* need before. But my parents are different. Our family is different. It feels foreign, being at home, and I never know what might spark some sort of massive argument that will last for days. I never know when I'll walk past the guest room and hear Mom trying to stifle her sobs.

I pull off the highway to a rest stop where I grab some chicken noodle soup in a cup, two bags of chips, a Gatorade, and some beef jerky. Then, I hop back in my car and drive the last few miles, over Meade Bridge, and onto Big Moon Drive.

When I pull up to Aunt Winnie's, all the lights are out but one. It's almost dark now, but when I get out, I hear the rhythmic sounds of something heavy crashing into something heavier over and over again.

When I walk around to the backyard, the last of the sunlight is bright on the water, making me shield my eyes.

And then I see him, wailing away at a piece of wood with an axe. He doesn't *look* sick.

He sees me and does a double take. The axe slides down in his hand a bit. His shaggy hair is disheveled, and there's sweat on his eyebrow even though it's freezing outside.

His eyes widen a bit when he sees me, and he looks down at the ground in shame. He walks up the back hill toward me.

"Hey," he says, looking at me with guilty eyes.

"Hi," I say.

"So, I guess you can see I'm not really sick," he says with a shrug. I nod slowly. He takes a breath and tosses the axe to the side. His eyes find mine again, and I see so much pain behind them that I almost can't handle it. I take a step closer to him and stick my hand out. I don't care why he didn't come. I just know that he needs me right now. So, here is where I'm going to be.

He draws in a breath, takes my hand, and pulls me into him. He wraps his arms around me so tight, my head against his chest, and breathes me in, his lips pressed against my head.

"I'm sorry I didn't tell you the truth," he whispers. I swallow and take a step backward.

"I know you must have had a good reason," I tell him. He looks down at me and turns his head to the side, using a finger to brush a piece of hair behind my ear.

"How is it that of all the guys in the world, you picked me?" he whispers. My stomach flips, and I give him a nervous smile as I pluck a piece of hair to start twirling. Then, he pulls me into him again, and this time, his grasp is desperate, like he's worried I'm going to run away. It lasts long, this embrace, but I don't mind. It feels like every piece of my chaotic life is frozen in space right now. That none of it matters; it's just white noise.

Until I feel his shoulders shuddering. And I realize my saving grace is standing here in my arms, sobbing.

"Hey, hey," I whisper, trying to pull him back so I can see his eyes. At first, he doesn't budge. Then, he sinks to the ground, and I follow suit.

For a minute, we sit there, his face pressed against my shoulder, his tears soaking through the fabric of my sweatshirt. Meade Lake winters are *cold,* and I had forgotten just *how* cold until we're kneeling in the snow.

Finally, he looks up at me, his cheeks tear-stained, his emerald eyes bloodshot.

I cup his face in my hands and look into them.

"What is going on?" I ask him.

He hangs his head and drops back on his butt in the snow. He wipes his cheek on his sleeve and looks out across the frozen water.

"It's my mom," he finally says. I look at him.

"What about her?"

"She's leaving," he says. I'm confused. She leaves all the time.

"For how long?" I ask.

"For good," he says. My heart is beating a million miles a minute.

"What? What do you mean for good?"

He shrugs and leans back on his arms.

"She called Aunt Winnie tonight. Said she's never felt more 'at home' than she does in San Diego. Met some guy," he says. "So she's staying."

"But...what about you?" I ask. "Are you...are you going out there?" I know he needs me, but as humans typically do, I can't help but think about me. About *us*. *Am I losing him?*

He lets out this little chuckle that's oozing with irony.

"Nope," he says. "It wasn't even an option."

"You mean...she didn't ask?"

He shakes his head.

"Nope," he says. "Asked Aunt Winnie if I could finish out my senior year here. Apparently, she feels that she hasn't really 'lived' since she had me. She feels it's time."

Now my heart is breaking for him, splintering behind my rib cage.

My parents are a lot of things—manipulative, preoccupied, oblivious. But there's not a bone in my body that doubts that either of them would give up their lives in less than a second for my brother or me.

I know they don't want each other, but there's not a doubt in my mind that they want *me*. I can't imagine what that would feel like.

"Oh, Ryder," I whisper, reaching out and putting my hand on top of his.

"I've always known that she would take off as soon as she could, as soon as she was ready," he says. "I just never thought it would be before *I* was ready. But then, I guess, are you ever ready to feel unwanted?"

"Hey," I say. I scoot across the snow, my extremities completely numb at this point. I reach out and cup his face in my hands again. He pushes back up onto his knees so that we're facing each other again.

"As long as I'm here, you will be wanted for the rest of your life," I tell him. And although I recognize those words carry a *lot* of weight for us being a couple of high schoolers, I know that there's not a point in my life where I will think I didn't mean them, even if it was just for this moment.

19

I pull his truck into the driveway of my house just as the last bit of daylight is fading away. I could tell he wasn't really in a place to drive when we were at the top of the mountain. I turn the ignition off, but neither of us move. His head is against the headrest, and he's staring blankly out the windshield.

"I don't know how to do this," he whispers, pinching the bridge of his nose with his thumb and index finger. "God, Annabelle. If I don't…"

I reach my hand out and take his in mine, interlocking our fingers.

"Annabelle is going to be fine. With her father," I tell him. "Come inside. I texted Derrick, and they are covering for you at Lou's. Alma is going to keep Annabelle tonight. You hungry?"

He turns his head to me, and after a second, a little smile tugs at his lips, and he nods. I can feel myself melting.

He follows me inside, and when he's in, he stops and looks around. I realize he hasn't been inside of this house since before everything happened. I pause to watch him, wondering what memories are crashing into him right now.

His eyes travel across the great room and up the big, A-frame windows.

"Memories, huh?" I ask him, leaning against the island. His eyes find me, and he nods.

"Uh, yeah," he says, scratching the back of his head. I wave him into the kitchen and motion for him to take a seat at the island while I pull out ingredients for home-made pizza.

"Man," he says, "speaking of memories. Glad to see your taste hasn't changed too much, because I haven't had a Walton pizza in *way* too long."

I smile.

"They've gotten a little more gourmet over the years," I say, rolling out the dough that I had in the fridge. He laughs.

"Beer?" I ask without thinking. Can cancer patients drink beer? I have no idea what the rules are. And that scares the shit out of me.

But he nods, so I reach back into the fridge, pop the top off, and slide it across the granite.

"So, your parents still rent this place out?" he asks. I nod.

"If it didn't make so much money in rentals, he would have sold it long ago," I say. "I think, originally, they thought they'd always have it in the family, ya know? Pass it down to Chase and me."

Silence.

"Then, maybe one day, our kids. But seeing as how none of that can happen now, I imagine they will sell it one day when it's too hard to manage."

He cocks his head. I know he's wondering why me not having kids is such a definite. I know he knows about my miscarriage. But he doesn't know the rest. I wipe my hands off on a towel and walk toward the foyer. I reach into my bag on the front table and pull out my notebook. I flip to the next letter and tear it out. I walk it back to him slowly, my hand shaking. And I hand it over, quickly returning to the pizza while he reads.

Ryder,

Three miscarriages in, one with a full D&C, and today marks the official two-year anniversary of starting fertility treatments.

It's funny. I remember when we were kids, talking about our first time, and how we considered using two condoms because we thought it would be double the protection. Come to find out, I couldn't have gotten pregnant if I tried.

The doctors finally mentioned the "A" word today: adoption. They told me not to get down, and that pregnancy can still happen for me. But that we can "always consider adoption." Yes, I know that. I just was hoping that my own fucking body would work the way it was designed to.

Luke's so patient. He's so kind. These hormones make me such a jackass, and combined with my stress levels, I don't know how he's surviving. But he is. He's such a good man. He loves me so much.

But every time something like this happens, every time there's more bad news, I can see it in his eyes how much he's hurting. He wants to be a dad.

He deserves more.

Mila

There's a long beat, the silence deafening while he reads. Then I hear the barstool he's sitting on scoot across the hardwood, and I hear his footsteps coming up from behind. He gently places his hand on top of mine, stopping me from sprinkling the cheese. With his other hand, he grabs my wrist and spins me toward him. Slowly, I lift my eyes to him.

He leans forward, reaching a hand out to cup the side of my face. I swallow, the sensation of his skin on mine still sending off a fire through my veins.

"You are enough," he says. "You are more than enough. And if ever there's an idiot who tells you differently, you should run in the other direction."

For the record, Luke never told me differently. He told me exactly what Ryder is telling me. But it felt a little different coming from him. It felt a little less true.

"And someday, somehow, you *will* be a mom, Mila. Because it's what you were meant for," he whispers. I don't realize I'm tearing up until he slides his thumb up to swipe one away.

I wake up on the big couch in the great room, the sun streaming in through the big glass doors. There's nothing but a few pieces of crust left on the pizza pan and a few empty beer bottles on the end table next to me. Across my lap is one of his long legs, hooked underneath mine. I look down and see that we're holding hands, and my heart swells.

He starts to stir as I try—and fail—to sneak out from underneath him.

"Hey," he says sleepily, stretching and pushing himself up off the couch.

"Hey yourself," I say back. After the moment in the kitchen last night, we lightened the mood some by stuffing ourselves with food and beer, laughing and talking on the couch and out on the deck.

A few times, our hands touched, our shoulders skimmed one another.

But nothing else.

I don't know when, or how, or if I should make another move. All I know is, I *want* to.

"Coffee?" I ask, tucking a piece of hair behind my ear nervously. He smiles as he pushes himself up. He doesn't say anything to me; he just takes a few steps toward me. When he gets to me, he pushes another piece of hair back off my face.

"I always wanted to know what it would be like to see you first thing in the morning," he says, and my cheeks flush. I laugh nervously and hold my hand out.

"Well, now you know," I say. "A rat's nest on my head, smeared mascara, and probably drool stains."

He smiles.

"Perfect," he says.

"So, about that coffee," I say, starting toward the kitchen. He follows me in with a handful of trash and all of our dishes from the night before.

"I actually need to get going. I gotta pick up my girl," he says with a smile. "Are you still up for meeting her today?"

I swallow and smile.

"Nothing else I want to do more," I tell him. He smiles, and my legs become gelatin beneath me.

"Come around lunchtime?" he asks, headed for the door. I smile and nod.

After all that's happened here the last month or so, my nerves have been on a roller coaster on the daily. But no encounter with Ryder measures up to the anxiety stirring inside of me thinking about meeting his four-year-old daughter.

I want her to like me.

I'm scared she won't.

I want him to *see* that she likes me.

I'm scared he won't.

But I don't want to fall in love with this little girl who is half some wonderful unicorn of a woman I'll never know, and half the person who has molded my world more than any other human.

I'm scared I will.

After cleaning up the kitchen for the second time and taking a shower, I realize I still don't have a bathing suit. I've got a little less than an hour until I'm going to head over there, so I decide to head up to town to grab a suit from the shop and something from the market that a kid would like. Kids can be easily swayed with something sweet, and I'm not above some bribery.

I use my keys to get into the back door of the shop and head for the back storage room where I know we keep the extra swimsuits.

I find a rack of women's suits and start spinning it around.

There are full wetsuits, one-pieces, a few things with frills, and some basic bikinis.

I find a navy bikini in my size and pull it off the rack. I strip down and try it on, tying it around my back and looking at myself in the long mirror that hangs on the back of the door. The bottoms are a little cheekier than I would like, but I've been working out a good amount, and I guess it wouldn't be the worst thing in the world if a little more hung out.

Just as I'm spinning around, checking out my ass, the door bursts open.

"Oh, shit!" Ryder calls out, the stack of boxes he's

carrying crashing to the ground. I jump back and let out a little yelp.

"I'm sorry," he says, bending down slowly to pick up the boxes. "We got an email that a big shipment was being dropped off today, so I just wanted to get it inside before I picked her up."

"I just, um, I forgot about the suit, so I came up to try one out," I say. He stands back up, and as he does, his eyes scour my body on their way up back to mine.

He takes a few steps closer to me, reaching behind my head to put one of the boxes on the shelf behind me.

"That one is a good choice," he whispers mere inches from my ear. "See you soon." Then he ducks back out of the room.

I smile and bite my lip as I give myself one more glance in the mirror.

I change back into my clothes, put the suit in my bag, and grab a towel out of a box next to me. I stop at the market and grab some carrots and hummus, a bottle of wine—obviously, for the adults—and about six different kinds of candy bars. I also grab a big bag of popcorn in case she's the savory type. In the checkout line, I see a sparkly butterfly balloon, and I grab that, too.

I pull onto Big Moon Drive and drive down to the end of it where I see a few cars have already made their way up. I hop out of my car and reach over the console to grab the goods from my passenger seat. As my ass is sticking out of the side of my car, I hear someone whistle in my direction. I scoot out quickly and turn around.

Luna Peake.

It's been over a decade, and yet, she hasn't aged. The same long, straight, black hair. The same fierceness about her. But still the biggest smile.

"Luna?" I ask. She runs to me and wraps her arms around me.

"So the rumors *are* true," she says, giving me an extra squeeze.

"What rumors?" I ask.

"That you're back in Meade Lake," she says. "And back with…" She nods her head toward the house. I clear my throat and tuck a piece of hair behind my ear. I should correct her. Shouldn't I? We're not…together. Are we?

"How have you been?" I ask, evading the subject completely. She smirks.

"Ah, you know. Still fighting the good fight. Trying to keep these bastards off my mountain," she says with a shrug. I nod. Luna's family were some of the first inhabitants of the Meade Lake area. Her mother is Native American, descendant of the original tribes that lived here. Her family still owns part of Meade Mountain, but it appears, judging by the development at the top of it, they're losing it piece by piece.

"I'm sorry, Luna," I say. "Keep it up."

She nods.

"Are you still with…" I start to ask, but she bursts out laughing.

"Daniel?" she blurts out. "Girl, no. We broke up shortly after you…after you stopped coming around. Turns out, he was the giant asshole everyone told me he was. Young love can be dumb love, though."

I smile, then I turn to the house in front of us.

"But young love can also be real," she says, elbowing

me gently. I smile back. I'm starting to see now, more every day that I'm here, just how true that is. It's terrifying.

We head inside, but most people are out back. There are a few people in the kitchen, and I immediately recognize Derrick's mom, Alma, at the stove. She's using tongs to pull cobs of corn out, and Miss May is standing next to her, holding a big tray, catching the cobs as she tosses them in.

They look up at us as we walk further into the house.

"Well, now, look who the cat dragged in!" Alma calls out to Luna, who puts a bag of dinner rolls that she brought on the counter and then leans down to kiss Alma's cheek. She scoots to the side and does the same to May.

"You all remember—"

"Mila Walton," Alma says, putting a hand on her hip. "It's been, what, thirteen, fourteen years?" she asks with a smile. I smile back as I walk to her with open eyes.

"Don't age me, Miss Alma," I say. "It's only been twelve. Miss May, it's so good to see you, too."

"It's so nice to see you after all these years, honey," May says with her familiar, warm smile.

"How are your parents?" Alma asks. I swallow and nod.

Still miserable. Still pretending not to be.

"Just as good as always," I say with a fake smile. *Lie.* "Happily retired now." *Nothing happy about it.*

"That's wonderful," she says with a warm smile. "I think about them every now and then. You, too."

You mean you think about my dead brother.

"Well, head on out back, girls; that's where all the fun is," Alma says, pointing us toward the back doors.

I follow Luna out the back door, and the deck and yard are scattered with a few people, some of whom I recognize. Teddy is down on the lawn with a little boy, swinging him around and putting him back down. There are a few more kids running up and down the yard in their bathing suits, screaming and laughing as they jump into the water.

Derrick is at the grill, flipping burgers and laughing with a few others.

I hear a loud shriek, and I look back out to the water where I see Ryder. He's standing at the edge of the dock, hoisting one of the kids above his head while the others laugh with joy in the water below. They join him in counting to three, and then Ryder launches the kid into the lake. His brown locks are slicked back to his head, wet with lake water. The sun sticks to the droplets on his bare chest, and I can't help but stare at him.

He doesn't *look* sick. In fact, in this beautiful moment, he looks very, *very* healthy.

He smiles when he sees me then jogs off the edge of the dock and up the back hill to the house.

"You made it," he says. The closer he gets, the more I want to reach out and touch his skin, feel that familiar shock of flesh on flesh that I only ever have with him.

"I did," I say with a smile. "Oh, and I brought a suit."

His eyes widen with delight, and one corner of his mouth tugs up.

"Excellent," he says, devilish half-grin still lingering. "So, you ready?"

"For what?" I ask. Then, like clockwork, off in the distance, a high-pitched, sing-song voice calls his name.

"Daddy!"

Our heads whip in unison.

And then I see her for the first time.

Annabelle Elizabeth Casey. The most beautiful little creature I've ever laid my eyes on.

She has these brown curls with golden streaks—something she got from her mom, I'm assuming. She has tan skin and green eyes, and I know those are from her dad. Her sparkling eyes meet mine, and I feel my heart skip a beat.

I've been a kid person my whole life. I love them. I'm drawn to them. I'm the woman at the grocery store ooh-ing and ahh-ing at every infant and toddler I see.

But there's something more about this little girl. I think it's that half of her comes from the person who has had the longest-lasting imprint on my life. I think it's because the moment I see her, I see him.

She's wearing a hot-pink bathing suit. Her little toes are painted pink, and when she reaches for Ryder's hand, I see that her fingernails match.

"When are you coming in the water with me?" she asks him. She's tugging on his hand, looking up at him then slowly bringing her eyes to me. When I smile at her, she quickly diverts them back to him and tucks herself behind his leg.

I kneel down in front of her so we're eye to eye.

Ryder does the same.

"This is her, Annabelle," he whispers to her. I have butterflies in my stomach. "This is who I told you about this morning. Remember? Mila."

She brings a finger to her mouth and chews on it thoughtfully as she nods.

"Hi, Annabelle," I say softly. "I'm so excited to meet you." She stares at me, still chewing on her finger. "Listen, I brought you a few things. I'm not sure what you like, but I brought a few treats. If your dad is okay with it, that is."

He gives me a devilish smile and nods.

"Do you want to come check them out?" I ask her. She nods, and before I realize it, she lets go of his hand and takes mine, leading me to the house. I turn back for a moment, just long enough to see him narrow his eyes at us, the most light I've seen in them since he got the news.

She chooses the popcorn, and I make a note that she's a savory snack kind of kid. She's obsessed with the balloon and has started to show it to every person at the house. He comes up behind me, and he's so close I can feel the heat from his body.

"Been here for five minutes, and you're already a hit," he whispers in my ear. It sends chills down my neck and arms.

"She's incredible, Ryder," I tell him, watching her as she shows Alma her balloon for the third time. Every soul in the room lights up when she approaches them. Every person in the yard stops what they are doing to listen to her.

"That's all her mom," he says, and I follow his gaze back to her. I smile and nudge him with my shoulder.

"Maybe not *all* of it," I say. The corner of his mouth tugs up, and he looks at me. He scoots a little closer to me on the deck.

"Care to test out that new suit?" he whispers, and a

zap goes through my body. I feel heat in places that have long since been heatless. I look at him, and he looks like he's waiting—scared, almost—for my reaction. But I just smile.

"Where can I change?"

A few minutes later, I'm walking down the backyard toward the water where the rest of the party has gathered. May and Alma are on the shore, drinking lemonade and chatting in two Adirondack chairs. Almost everyone else is in the water. I hear a shriek, and I see Ryder tossing Annabelle into the air and catching her. As I get closer, they turn to me.

"Come in, Mila, come in!" she says, pushing her soaked curls out of her angelic little face.

"Yeah, come in, Mila," he says with a grin. He lifts her up onto the dock, and she takes off toward shore, toward me. But she doesn't see the plank that's sticking up. Her toe clips it, and it sends her flat to her face.

Before I realize, I'm on my knees in front of her, scooping her up and carrying her off the dock. She's skinned and scared.

"Hey, hey," I whisper as Alma and Ryder are rushing to us. "Can I take a look?"

She nods reluctantly, the crocodile tears sailing down her cheeks, hitting me like a punch to the gut.

I sit her on my lap and take a look at her hands and knees.

"We should get some peroxide on those, baby," Alma says.

"Let's get you inside, kiddo," Ryder says, kneeling down to grab her. But she shakes her head, wrapping her arms around my neck.

"I want Mila to carry me," she says. I look to Ryder, and a slow smile spreads on his lips.

"Let's go, honey," I say, scooping her back up and carrying her inside.

After some dramatics in the kitchen while Alma cleaned her cuts and bandaged them up, we're back on the deck. She's on my lap with a popsicle, and Ryder is just looking at us from across the big wooden table.

The crowd is slowly dwindling, but Luna and a few others are still down by the water. When Annabelle is finally ready to make her reappearance, we venture back down to the shore.

"There she is!" Derrick calls out. "My big tough girl."

Annabelle smiles as she runs to him. He pops her up on his knee.

"Welcome back, kiddo," Teddy says. "You're almost as crazy as your dad. Someday, when you're big, we will tell you all the stories about your dad. He used to be a maniac on the water."

Everything goes quiet.

All eyes are on me, then on Ryder, then on me.

Teddy audibly swallows.

"Shit," he mutters quietly as Derrick shoots him a death glare.

My stomach flips when I make eye contact with Ryder. It feels cold and distant, like everything that's happened over the last two months is quickly evaporating into thin air. Conversation picks up again, and I feel like I am comfortably disappearing to the rest of the guests.

But not to him. He doesn't take his eyes off of me until Alma asks him to help her load up her car.

More people start to leave, and I take advantage of the commotion. I say a quick goodbye to everyone on the lawn, including Annabelle.

"Why are you leaving, Mila?" she asks me, and I melt where I stand.

"I have to go home to my house," I tell her.

"Can I see you tomorrow?" she asks me. I melt again.

"I'll have to check with your daddy, honey," I tell her. "But I'll make sure I see you soon, okay?"

She thinks for a moment and bites her little lip. Then, she takes a step back and leaps into my arms, wrapping her little ones around my neck. She buries her face into me, and I feel nothing but euphoria. I hold her tight for a moment longer then let her go to play with Teddy's kids.

I look around once more then slink off the side of the house.

"I'm sorry my brother's an idiot," Derrick says, scaring the shit out of me as I reach for my handle.

"Oh!" I say. "Jesus. You scared me. It's...it's fine."

He smiles.

"It's fine? That why you're sneaking off without saying goodbye to him?"

I chew the inside of my cheek.

"I just...I need a little space," I tell him. He thinks for a moment then nods. He comes to me and wraps me in a quick hug.

"Get home safe," he says. I nod, get in my car, and speed back to my house.

He was a maniac on the water.

20

THEN, SUMMER BEFORE SENIOR YEAR

We've been here for four weeks already, and I have seen Ryder all but one day when we had to go home for a mayoral event, and he had to work a night shift at the diner.

I thought last summer was the best of my life so far, but I was wrong.

Waking up knowing I'll see him, lying on the dock with him, dipping our toes in the water, hanging with our friends in the evenings.

I cannot think of a time where everything felt so perfectly still. Like time is frozen just how it should be. We made it through our first year of being apart like it was cake. We visited, video called, texted, and actually sent letters. My mother was shocked that kids still did that.

And perhaps the sweetest part of our relationship is the friendship that's grown between Ryder and Chase. A few of the weekends Ryder visited us during the school year, he and Chase played basketball and saw movies. I was only allowed to come to Meade Lake when they knew Aunt Winnie would be home—little did they know that even when she was "home," she was hardly ever at the house—and a few times, Chase came with me. He and Ryder would fish early in the mornings, and the three of us would go out on the boat in the evenings.

It feels like all is well with the world now that we're back here. I can get back to avoiding the issues of my parents; I can stop fake smiling at Dad's mayoral events and start *actually* smiling again. At least, for the summer.

And I know I'm only seventeen, but I know that I love this boy. I know that, one day, I might look back and realize it wasn't the same kind of love that can stand the test of time. I don't know what our future holds, but I know that, in this moment, this summer, at this lake, he is mine. He has my heart, and I don't want it back.

"Whatcha readin'?" he asks me, poking his head around my shoulder and landing a kiss on my cheek. I smile and nuzzle into him as he grabs the chair next to me on the back deck. He and Chase just got back from their morning fishing session.

"This book that Jules let me borrow," I tell him. He grabs it and flips to the front cover.

"*And Then There Was You?*" he asks with a judgmental smile. I snatch it back and make a face. "What's it about?"

"It's about this girl," I tell him, "who moves to this lake town. She meets this dangerously handsome local boy." Suddenly, with his green eyes on me, I feel this zap of energy. I feel this desire, this heat that's been boiling below the surface for a year now.

He smirks and reaches out to grab the arms of my chair. He slowly whips my chair around and pulls it into him so that we're facing each other.

"Mhmm," he says. "Dangerously handsome, huh?"

I nod.

"Go on," he says.

"And the girl tries to hold herself back," I say, my voice dropping to a low whisper, "but all she really wants is to touch his body. Feel every single—"

He clears his throat and resituates himself in his chair.

I go on.

"Inch of him," I say. I watch his Adam's apple bob as he swallows. His eyes move slowly from my eyes, to my lips, down to my chest. His tongue juts out to wet his lips, and then he slowly looks back up to me.

We haven't explicitly talked about it yet, but I think the possibility of sleeping together is hanging over both of us. I never had much of an interest in it before now. Before him.

But my body aches—in a good way—for him, different than I've ever felt before. He's so gentle, so delicate, like he's afraid I'm going to crumble into dust and blow away from him. It's still endearing, how he is with me, but in some ways, like having his whole body to myself, I'm ready for more. I'm ready to not be so delicate.

I push myself up from my chair and stand between his legs, looking down at him. He parts them slightly so that I can get even closer. I take his face in my hands and look into his big green eyes. He swallows audibly again, and I think this is the first time I've ever seen him nervous.

"I want this with you," I tell him flat out.

He swallows again and puts his hands on my hips,

pulling me in even closer. He looks around, making sure none of my family is within earshot.

"Mila, I want it with you, too. But I don't want you to feel like—"

"I don't feel like anything, except that I want you."

That dangerous half-smile creeps onto his lips.

"Then you have me," he says. I smile and kneel down for another one of the sweetest kisses I'm sure I will ever have in my life. I look around now.

"My parents go back to Kelford tonight for some dinner. I'm sure Chase will make plans," I tell him, raising my eyebrows. He reaches a hand up and strokes my bottom lip with his thumb, leaving a trail of heat in its wake.

"Tonight it is," he says.

"Yo, who wants burgers?" Chase calls from the side of the house as he walks up the deck steps. Ryder smiles at me.

"We do," he says, hopping up and taking my hand. As we follow Chase toward his truck, Ryder lifts my hand to his lips and kisses it.

WHEN WE GET to the boardwalk, the gang's all there, already chowing down. Jules and Kirby are playing volleyball on the grass by the water against Teddy and Derrick. From the looks of it, the guys are struggling to keep up. When they see us grabbing a table, they finish up their game and make their way up to us.

"Hey, guys," Ryder says, grabbing a few extra chairs and sliding them up to the table. He sinks down in the chair next to me and puts his hand on my thigh. I look around at the other people around us—mostly vacationers, families, a few groups of kids around our age—and think about how happy I am to have found this group of people.

To not be a visitor this time, to really feel like I'm home.

I think about what life will look like down the line for Ryder and me.

Maybe it'll look a lot like this moment right now: hanging out with our favorite people, our fingers intertwined, in our favorite place. Our home.

After a little while, we run low on fries. I volunteer to go order more at the window. Ryder offers to go for me, but he's not done with his burger, so I tell him I'll go.

I'm one person away from reaching the counter when I can feel someone close in behind me. I feel the brush of fabric against my body.

"You're not a local, are you?" a deep voice asks. I turn around to face him—a tall, bronzed guy that looks to be around our age.

"Sorry?" I ask.

"I see you hanging out with that crew a lot, but you're not from Meade Lake, are you?" he asks.

I give him a look, and he chuckles.

"It's easy to spot the out-of-towners," he says. He sticks out a long, slender hand. "I'm Ricky. I go to school with *those* animals."

I shake his hand hesitantly. I turn to place my order, but he cuts me off.

"Nah, give her the onion rings instead of the fries, Carlos," he calls through the window. "She doesn't know what she's missing. And put it on my tab," he says with a wink that almost makes me cringe. And I hate onion rings.

"Uh, I'm good, thank you. I actually will take those fries," I say through the window, sliding a five dollar bill in. Carlos smiles at me then slides a carton of fries out to me.

I look up at Ricky, and he smirks at me.

"A lady that knows what she wants. I like it," he says. He takes a step closer to me, then another, until I'm flush up against the food truck. I glance over at the table, but it doesn't seem like Ryder or Chase has noticed yet. I swallow. *I'm fine. We're in public.*

I shimmy out from his overbearing shadow and slide over to the condiment counter. I pour some ketchup into a plastic cup then go to turn back to the tables. But Ricky steps in front of me.

"So, listen, some friends and I were gonna go out on the water tonight. I'd love to show you the lake," he says.

"Thanks, but I'm out on the water all the time," I say, taking a step around him. But he blocks me again, this time reaching for my arm. I can't help but notice his grip around my wrist. He doesn't strike me as dangerous or forceful, but he strikes me as someone who normally gets his way. Especially with girls.

"Not like this you haven't," he says with a smile. "Not with a local."

"Actually," I say, "my boyfriend is a local. I get the local tour quite often."

He cocks his head and lifts an eyebrow.

"Boyfriend?" he asks.

"Boyfriend," Ryder says from behind him, making Ricky jump slightly. I bite my lip to keep from smiling.

"You date Casey?" Ricky asks, jutting a thumb out toward Ryder.

"I do," I say.

Chase appears next to him and lifts his elbow to Ryder's shoulder.

"She does. So we're good here. Thanks, Romeo," he says, reaching out to take the carton of fries and turning on his heel. I smile to myself. My boys have my back.

Ryder reaches a hand out for me—one I take gladly—and I scurry away from Ricky's reach. We turn to walk away when Ricky calls his name.

"When are we getting back on the water?" he asks him. Ryder's eyes grow wide. He looks down at me then looks back to Ricky.

"We're not," he tells him. Ricky scoffs.

"Still got a bad taste in your mouth from the last time?" he asks with a smile. I look up at Ryder, wondering what I'm missing.

"Something like that," he says, snaking his arm around my shoulders and leading Chase and me back to the table.

"We'll be out there tonight, Casey," Ricky calls. "If you decide you wanna stop being a pussy and redeem yourself."

I can feel Ryder's muscles tense, but he doesn't turn back to Ricky. He just keeps walking toward our tables.

"What is he talking about?" I ask when we're out of Ricky's earshot.

"Yeah, what was that about?" Chase asks.

"Ah, it's nothing. We used to race when we were younger," Ryder says with a casual wave of his hand.

"Race?" Chase asks, and I see this little flame ignite in his eyes. My brother, the eternal thrill seeker.

"Out by the dam, we used to race our boats. Real stupid," Ryder says. "I don't do it anymore."

"Why not?" Chase asks.

"We almost crashed once," Ryder says, unable to lift his eyes to mine. "So I stopped. When I met you."

I swallow, my heart rate picking up. I squeeze his hand.

WHEN WE GET BACK to the table, Jules and Luna are standing up and pulling their purses over their shoulders.

"Where ya goin'?" Ryder asks.

"We were gonna run to the bookstore in Oakton," Luna says. "You wanna come, Mila?"

A new book does sound good. And I have been missing some female bonding.

"You guys are such nerds," Shane says. "Books over the summer."

Jules picks up a fry and chucks it at him. He catches it and pops it into his mouth. They exchange this smile, and I feel something between them. They act like siblings sometimes, noogies and playful shoving, bickering over plans. But there's something between them.

"We have to get attached to fictional men since the ones we hang out with are so lame," she says with a smirk.

I look to Ryder.

"Now we can fish," Chase says, slapping Ryder on the back. Ryder smiles at me and kisses my cheek.

"Go. Have fun," he says. I smile and kiss him back. As I pull away, he whispers in my ear.

"But tonight is mine," he says. I bite my lip then scoot out from the table.

. . .

Shopping is fun, and I can't remember ever getting along so well with two other girls. They are so laid back, so genuine. I smile at Luna's stories about growing up on the mountain and at the way Jules can't help but bring Shane up.

Yeah, definitely something there.

Jules helps me pick out a few new romance novels, and Luna settles for a new cookbook she's had her eye on for a few weeks.

"You know," Luna says after a few minutes of silence on Lakeside Highway, "I've never seen Ryder Casey like this over any girl."

"Like what?" I ask sheepishly.

"I don't know," she says. "Like he can't live without you."

I swallow.

"Me either, come to think of it," Jules says. "He's different. He moves a little slower. Takes his time a little more. It's cool." She smiles, and so do I.

I hope he will always take his time when it comes to me, because I want every second he will give me.

It's dark now, and I suddenly can't wait to get back to the house.

Tonight is mine.

We drive a few more minutes until we reach Lou's, and then the sky turns purple.

Blue and red lights flashing.

And the quiet night air is suddenly blaring with sirens. Cars are pulled over on the side of the road, and as we get closer, we see people standing everywhere, staring down at the water.

"What the fuck?" Luna says, pulling over next to the other cars. We all get out, and something in the air changes.

Jules is staring at the water, her mouth agape.

And then Luna is clued in to whatever Jules sees. Her eyes widen, and her mouth opens.

I look down at the water, the huge dam at the edge, now with a huge hole in it where a mangled boat is perched.

"Oh, my God," Jules says.

"Jules!" we hear Derrick say. He's down the hill, waving his hands to her. She swallows.

"Luna, stay here with Mila," she says, her eyes trained on Derrick.

I feel Luna's hand snake around mine, her grasp hard and firm, like she's afraid she'll lose me.

I see Derrick telling Jules something, and then I see her whole body start to shake. Derrick wraps his arms around her then lifts his eyes slowly to us. They walk back to us.

"Mila," Derrick says, his voice shaky and cracking, "that's...that's Ryder's boat."

I swallow, this loud buzz filling my ears and making it difficult to hear anything else.

I make out the words "Ryder and Chase" and "racing." I swallow, and my ears pop, and then I rest my eyes on Derrick.

"Mila, the police are trying to get in touch with your parents. Can you give me your phone so I can get it to them?" he asks. I'm on autopilot. I reach my hand down into my bag and hand my phone to him. He hands it to Jules, who takes off toward an officer. And then I come back down to earth.

"Oh, my God!" I scream, wriggling out of Luna's grasp, blowing past Derrick, and running toward the water.

Before I make it, I feel Derrick's strong arms wrap around me, pulling me back from the black water in front of us. People are staring as I scream and try desperately to escape his grasp, but I don't care. Luna is helping him hold onto me, and we all collapse onto the ground.

Derrick clutches me to his chest, and Luna squeezes my hand as tears fall from her eyes.

My heart is in two halves, and they were both on that mangled boat that's crashed into the dam.

By some sort of divine intervention, my parents had gotten in a fight before they left for home, so they had been late leaving. They were only twenty minutes outside of Meade Lake when they got the call.

Now, the three of us are sitting in the chairs of the ICU at Meade Hospital, wondering how the fuck we got here.

When my parents got to the scene earlier, the paramedics had just pulled Chase out of the water.

A police officer, an Officer Trout, had begun chest compressions until the paramedics arrived. They had gotten a weak pulse, threw an oxygen mask on him, and sped to the hospital.

When we got here, the doctor told us he coded twice on the way to the hospital. Both times, they were able to get his heart beating again. He was hooked up to a few other machines, and they were working on what sounded like every part of his body.

He has broken ribs, a broken wrist, and a broken femur, but what the doctors are most concerned about is the swelling in his brain.

None of us have spoken. We just sit here, staring blankly ahead, wondering how the fuck we got here.

A doctor comes out from the back, the solemn look on his face not exactly lifting my spirits.

"Chase has deep gashes in his head and on his face from when he was thrown from the boat into the brick wall of the dam. One of them was incredibly deep, and we're having trouble stopping the bleeding," he tells us. They weren't sure how much he'd lost at the scene, but they knew it was significant.

My dad and I look at each other and roll up our sleeves.

"All three of us have the same blood type," he tells the nurses.

"Unfortunately, it's not that kind of bleeding," the doctor says.

I ball my hands into fists and pound them onto my chair.

"He needs it. Take it!" I scream at him. My mother wraps her arm around my shoulders. The doctor drops his eyes to the ground, knowing there's nothing more to say.

"Mr. and Mrs. Walton," the doctor says, "we're doing everything we can, but Chase isn't responding. It might be best to go back with him. We will allow you and your daughter to be with him in the intensive care unit."

My parents both turn slowly to me. We all know that that's not a good sign.

"Come on, honey. Let's go back in there," Dad says to me.

But my legs feel like lead. I can't stand the look of Chase. Bloody, battered, swollen. Completely unrecognizable. I tell my parents to go ahead.

"I'll be in in a minute," I tell them.

I walk toward the edge of the waiting room, leaning up against the cool brick wall and inhaling slowly. I've been fighting off waves of nausea since I watched the paramedics push the stretcher carrying my brother's mangled body up the hill and load him into the ambulance. I close my eyes. I picture the last moments my eyes saw them both.

Ryder's big green eyes, smiling at me as he promised me the best night of my life. Chase's blue eyes that match my own. Then I picture the boat flying way too fast across the glass water. I imagine the sound it made when it crashed into the brick of the dam, like some sort of explosion.

"Mila?" I hear him ask, and suddenly, the blood running through my veins feels hot. I open my eyes slowly, and I see him standing there, awkwardly, a few feet away from me.

I see his Aunt Winnie in the corner of the waiting room, talking to a police officer.

My eyes trail back to Ryder, and I see his shirt covered in blood. My first instinct is to lunge for him, feel for a cut, ask if he's okay. But I'm frozen.

"It's...it's not mine," he says, looking down at the ground, realizing what I'm staring at. And then suddenly, I'm enraged.

"I know it's not yours," I say quietly, my eyes burning holes in his face. He can't look at me.

"Mila...I...what are they saying?" he asks cowardly, still looking down at the ground. I want to scream. Every ounce of energy in my body wants to pound him into the ground until he's as bloody and broken as Chase. But I can't. Because I don't know if Chase is going to live.

And there's also a small part of me that was terrified, at first, that the one who might not make it was Ryder.

Just as I'm about to speak, an alarm goes off, coming from Chase's room. I see a huge team of people rush in while a few more rush out.

I hear the beeping of machines and see the blinking of lights flashing on the door from the hallway.

There are a few seconds of quiet, and I hear one of the doctors mumble something.

Then I hear my mother scream.

And if I'm not mistaken, I hear a sob escape my dad's lips.

A moment later, I see the doctor and his team step out of the room. He's tugging off his bloody gown and rubbing a hand over his face.

I look at Ryder. My brother is dead. Ryder killed my brother.

His eyes grow wide, and he finally lifts them to mine.

"You did this," I whisper. I see tears welling in his eyes. "This is because of you."

"Mila, I'm..." he says, his lip trembling. Aunt Winnie is still watching us from the corner of the room, her hand covering her mouth. Suddenly, Ryder takes a step closer to me.

"Mila, I'm so sorry. I..." he says, and now, he's

reaching his hands out to me. I pound my fists against his chest, then jump back and scream.

"Don't touch me!" I call out. I can feel twenty heads turning to us, and I don't give a good goddamn about it. "You're a fucking murderer! He's dead because of *you!*"

But he doesn't stop. He takes a step closer to me, and in that moment, I realize he's trying to pull back. He's trying to stop time, reverse it. He wants to hold me. He wants to be the shoulder for me. He wants to fix my heart.

But he can't. Because he's the one who has totally shattered it beyond repair.

He takes one more step toward me, and I slap him so hard my hand stings.

"Don't come near me. Don't speak to me or my family again. You're dead to me, Ryder," I say, taking a step toward Chase's room. Then I turn to him once more, ready to deliver one final blow.

"I wish it were you instead."

21

I'm lying on one of the chaises out on the deck, wrapped in a thick blanket, staring up at the stars. The night air is chilly here, even in the thick of summer, and the sky is usually bright and clear.

I'm struggling with whether or not to let myself feel what I felt when I heard Teddy's words or to try and let it go.

These last few months with Ryder have been so much more than I ever imagined. A continuation of our story, albeit, a slow one. But it's been just the right pace.

Until now, that is.

Over the last few days, I've found myself unable to stop thinking about him. Unable to stop reminiscing about our earlier years when it wasn't so complicated for him to be my everything.

I think about his body, wonder about the parts of it that I haven't seen in years, wonder how much more of a man he's become, in every way, shape, and form.

I think about how comfy it was to feel him next to

me on the couch the other night and wake up to him the next morning. And how easily I could get used to that.

A creak in the deck steps makes me jump, and I turn to the side.

"I'm sorry," Ryder says, holding his hands up. "I didn't mean to scare you."

I let out the breath I was holding in, but I feel my heart rate immediately pick up.

"I just wanted to check on you," he says.

"Where's Annabelle?" I ask him.

"At Alma's. She really milked the whole skinned-knee thing and talked Alma into a sleepover."

I chuckle quietly and nod. I wrap my arms around myself and pull my feet up onto the chaise.

"Is it okay if I…" he starts to ask, motioning to the chaise lounge next to me. I nod again.

He sits on it sideways so that he's facing me. I clear my throat and awkwardly look out over the water. I can't bring myself to look at him, as much as I want to.

"Mila," he says just above a whisper. "Can we talk about what Teddy said?"

Damn, he's a straight shooter.

I take in a deep breath and turn to him slowly.

"Okay," I say sheepishly.

"I'm so sorry," he says. "He didn't mean anything by it; he just doesn't think sometimes before he speaks."

I nod and wrap my arms around myself tighter.

"It's fine," I say in the most unconvincing tone of voice possible. After a long, awkward silence, I scoot off the end of my lounge and walk toward the rail. I lean on it and look back over the water. There's so much I want to say to him, but it feels like my thoughts are frozen. Like all I can concentrate on is the moonlight bouncing off the black water and the fact that the once love of my life is four feet behind me.

"It's not fine," I hear him say softly. I can hear him slide off his chair, and in an instant, he's next to me at the railing. "Mila."

I slowly lift my eyes to him.

"It's *not* fine," he says, his green eyes pouring into mine. "Nothing that happened was fine. And nothing that hurts you or makes you remember your hurt...nothing that makes you think of what I did to you and your family is fine. Nothing I *did* was fine."

I'm speechless. I don't know what to say. I don't know how to feel about any of it. The only thing I'm sure about is how I feel about him, and it's fucking terrifying. I swallow.

"Why did you...why did you do it?" I ask the question I've been holding back all these years. His eyes widen.

"I didn't want to race them," he says, turning away from me slightly and grabbing onto the railing as he looks out over the water. "I remembered how you asked me specifically not to do anything crazy. I even walked off the dock, but when I turned back, Chase was getting on the boat. I thought you'd never forgive me if he went alone. But I guess, it turns out, I still did something unforgivable."

I swallow. I've never heard the full story. Only the crash.

"I had finally convinced him to let me take over, and I was going to come back in," he goes on. "But Ricky picked up speed and headed toward the dam, and Chase couldn't let up. He had this crazy intensity in his eyes; I'd never seen anything like it."

"Wait...what?" I ask, and I see his whole body stiffen. He stands straight as a board, staring out over the lake, afraid to look at me. "What did you say? *Chase* picked up speed?"

His knuckles grow white as he clenches onto the railing.

"Ryder," I say, taking a step toward him. He drops his head down. "Who was driving the boat?"

My voice is shaky and uncertain, but I'm staring at him, imploring him for an answer.

He clears his throat and lifts his head slowly.

"*Ryder*," I say again, firm and crisp. He turns toward me.

"Chase," he whispers, and my vision gets blurry. I stumble backward a few feet and grab hold of the railing myself. He takes a step toward me, but I hold a hand out, keeping him at bay.

This changes things.

This changes *everything*.

All this time, all these years, I blamed him for the crash.

For Chase's death.

For it all.

I hated him.

My heart is pounding in my chest so rapidly that I feel a little faint. My palms are sweating, and there's a giant lump in my throat that I can't keep down.

"Mila—" he starts, but I whip my head up to him once I've steadied myself.

"How...how could you let us all think it was you?" I ask him, my voice soft and quiet, still in shock. "You went to *court*, Ryder. You were eighteen. You could have gone to jail."

"I know," he says.

"Ricky...didn't he see you? Why didn't he tell anyone?"

"We sped past them before we got to the dam. They weren't near us when we crashed," he says just above a whisper. "The cops assumed it was me because it was my boat. And I just didn't correct them."

My eyes dart back and forth across his face, but he can't bring himself to look at me.

"But...*why?* Why would you let us all think you did it? Why would you let *me* think that?"

He swallows and then, finally, lifts his eyes to mine.

"Because I couldn't...I couldn't let you think it was his fault. I thought it might...I don't know. I thought it might hurt less, somehow, if it wasn't him behind the wheel. That if you had to blame someone, it might be easier for you to blame me, instead of him, since he wouldn't be here to take it."

I want to grab a hold of him and not let go, but at the same time, I want to scream at him.

"Mila, I would do anything to bring him back. I am so sorry you lost him," he whispers.

I feel so much inside of me the tears are stinging the back of my eyes.

All this time...

That's it—I know I've reached my boiling point.

"God, Ryder!" I call out, and I can tell I've startled him. He swallows, his eyes wide as he stares back at me.

I turn on my heel and storm back into the house. I reach under the front table and pull my bag up on top of it, digging through it for my notebook. He stares at me through the sliding glass door. I flip to the next letter and tear it out with force. I stomp back out onto the deck and slam it against his chest. He looks down at it then back at me.

"What is this?" he asks.

"Read it," I say.

He takes in a deep breath then slips the crinkled paper from my hand and turns it over.

Ryder,

It's been ten years.

Ten years since he left.

But it's also been ten years since you *left.*

Every day since then, I've had at least one thought of you.

And every day, when I think of you, I become terrified that I'll never stop.

Mila

His hand starts to tremble, and he lifts his eyes to me slowly. I take a step closer to him.

The tears are pricking, and I'm staring, wide-eyed, begging them not to fall.

But they don't listen.

"What you don't get is that I haven't just had to live without my brother all these years. I've had to live without you, too." And now the tears flow, and I know it's useless to try and stop them.

He slowly lowers the letter and drops it on the rail. He takes a step closer to me and slowly lifts his hands to my face. He cups it gently, stroking my cheeks with his thumbs, wiping the tears away. I close my eyes and let my body feel what it feels like with his skin on mine.

"Mila," he whispers, stepping closer. "I'm so...I'm so——"

"Shh," I tell him, opening my eyes slowly. "Don't say it again."

He takes a step closer to me and pulls my lips to his.

A bolt goes through my body, making my fingertips tingle.

"Mila," he whispers between kisses, "I'm here now, okay? I'm here now. And I'm so—"

But I don't let him speak again; I don't let him say he's sorry. All this time, I've blamed him for the worst loss of my life. And all this time, the blame hasn't been his to bear.

I press my body against his and wrap my arms around his neck. I slip my tongue into his mouth, and he pulls away with a gasp. He looks down at me, his eyes wide.

I nod to him, and he wraps his arms around my waist, pulling me as close to him as possible. My feet leave the ground as his arms squeeze around me; I can feel every muscle in them clenching.

He sits me down on the rail, holding me close to him.

He slows down a bit, pulling away to look at me. But there's a fire starting inside of me, and I'm not ready for it to burn out.

I widen my legs and pull him in between them then grab the collar of his shirt and pull him into me.

I kiss him hard, savoring the taste of him. It's been years, but he's still the most delicious thing I've ever tasted.

My tongue massages his, and as I pull away, I keep his bottom lip between my teeth gently. His eyes sparkle, and I can't remember the last time I've wanted someone the way I want him in this moment.

Actually, I can.

When I was seventeen, and he was eighteen.

When he had only *felt* certain places on my body. When he only teased how good it could be.

Before anyone had ever seen all of me. Before I'd given myself to someone completely.

And now it's all coming back to me: how badly I wanted him in every possible way.

I wrap my legs around his waist and pull his body into mine, slipping my fingers under the hem of his shirt.

I slide it up off his body, and I ogle at the perfection that is his chest. I trace every curve, every peak, and every valley with my fingers, and then I pull him into me to leave a trail of kisses across it. He drops his head back slowly then scoots me off the railing and carries me toward the door.

His hands grip my ass as he walks, and I squeeze my thighs around him tighter, grinding myself against him. We get to the island, and he sets me down again, stepping back to gently reach for my shirt. I slowly lift my hands up over my head and let him slide it off, the fabric leaving a trail of chills on my skin.

I reach up a hand to the clasp of my bra, our eyes on each other's. I swallow then unclasp it and let it slink down my arms.

He takes me all in then wraps his arms around me again.

"Oh, Mila," he whispers, "you're so beautiful."

"Ryder," I whisper as he kisses my neck, "take me into the bedroom."

He pulls back for a moment, staring down at me.

I see him swallow, and I can feel his heart beating against my hand.

"Are you sure?" he asks.

"Take me back there," I tell him, "and don't leave until morning."

Without waiting another second, he slides me off the counter and carries me up the big staircase in the middle of the room. He pushes open the door to the last room in the hallway, which was mine growing up. I take a moment to appreciate how well he remembers everything. But not *too* long of a moment, because he lays me on the bed and starts unbuttoning my jean shorts.

I wriggle around to try and help him, and they slide down my legs. He tosses them to the ground then reaches up and unbuttons his own. They slide down to the ground, and I can't help but stare at him again in all his glory. My God, he's stunning.

He crawls up the bed and leans down for another kiss—this time, slow and sweet.

I let my hand slide down his body and underneath the thick band of his boxers. The muscles in his arms bulge as he holds his weight off of me, but he drops his head when I find him and wrap my fingers around him.

I slide my hand up and down, watching as his eyes roll back with every stroke. I reach up and kiss his neck and grab hold of his thick hair. After a few more strokes, he pulls away, sliding down my body and taking my panties with him.

This is the first time in my life that I've been completely naked in front of Ryder Casey, and it feels oddly surreal. I guess that's because I thought, for over a decade, that the window to this opportunity had been closed. Man, am I glad it's opening again.

He pushes himself back up, trailing his fingers up the inside of my thighs and stopping when he gets to my center. As he looks down at me, he slowly pushes one finger inside of me, then another. I claw for the sheets, pushing my head back against the bed. I'm wet and ready for him, and judging by the low moan escaping his lips, I know he can tell.

"Ryder," I whisper.

He pumps his fingers in and out, slowly at first, then picks up the pace as my hips buck toward him. I reach up and tug at his boxers, and he finally obliges, stepping back and pulling them down. I feast my eyes on him— all of him—and I feel like I'm about to boil over. The sight of him makes my legs spread wider, willing him to bring himself closer.

He crawls up the bed slowly, his eyes scouring my body until they meet mine.

"Mila," he whispers again before he bends down to kiss my lips again. "Mila, I need you."

"I'm yours, Ryder," I tell him, and I surprise myself. But the more the air around us clears, the more I realize I mean it. I *am* his. And I think that, all along, there was a part of me that never stopped being his.

And it's glorious, and exciting, and terrifying all at the same damn time.

Because a year from now, he might not be here. I might not have him, and this time, it won't be by choice.

I shake my head to focus on him, soaking in his body, his broad chest sprinkled with specks of hair, his green eyes shining in the moonlit room, his biceps flexed and braced around me.

He's always been beautiful as long as I've known him, but there's something about him right now that's making it impossible to focus on anything else. He's breathtaking, and raw, and vulnerable, but he's also the strongest person I've ever seen.

He bends down again, letting his fingers trace my lips once more.

With that, he pushes himself into me, and my whole body reacts to the feeling of his length in me, his fingers running through my hair, his warm body on top of mine. We move slowly at first, and then I feel my body spiraling out of control, like it's begging him for more.

"Ryder, please," I whisper as I dig my nails into his back, "please don't stop."

He moans as he moves faster, and I feel such intense pleasure that I feel dizzy.

"Mila," he says breathlessly, and it makes my head spin faster. I wrap my arms and legs around him, making the silent wish that these moments could last till the end of time.

22

I wake to him leaving a trail of soft kisses across my shoulders, and goosebumps rise all over my skin. His arms are wrapped around me tight, and I'm squinting in the sunlight that's creeping in through my bedroom window. I moan with delight as I push myself back into him, nestling into his grasp even more. If I had to define paradise, I'm pretty sure it'd be this moment, right here, with him.

"Morning," he whispers in my ear, his voice scruffy.

"Morning," I say, turning on my side so we're nose to nose. "Did you sleep okay?"

He smiles and pushes a stray piece of hair from my face.

"The best I've slept in years."

Despite the fact that he saw me naked last night— more than once—and despite the fact that I'm *still* currently naked, I still blush.

"Me, too," I tell him, running a finger down his nose and tracing his lips.

"I have to go to the shop today," he says, burying his face in my hair.

"Nooo," I say, pushing my bottom lip out. He kisses it and strokes my hair.

"I'm sorry," he says. "I want to help Derrick out as much as I can before…"

Suddenly, the air in the room gets cold and thick.

"Before I can't help as much," he finishes. I pull him in for one more long kiss and then nod. I watch as he slides out of the bed, his perfect ass taut as he strolls across the room to grab his clothes. He leaves the bathroom door open as he dresses, and I can't keep my eyes off of him. Every curve of his muscles, every dip of his abs, is braced as he pulls his shirt on and covers them.

All these years I've spent hating him. All this wasted time. We never got to finish our story because of a lie.

And now, we might not get to again.

I shake my head and clear my mind of the most impossible thoughts.

It's funny, I've gone so long hoping—planning—on never seeing him again. And now, I can't imagine going another day without seeing him.

He comes back out and crawls onto the bed, lying on top of me and putting an arm on either side of my head. He bends down to kiss my forehead, then my cheek, then my lips. I run my fingers through his dark locks, clutching onto him. I let my legs sneak around his, and he smiles and pulls away.

"You're trying to make me late, aren't you?" he asks. I smile.

"Maybe," I shrug. "I don't know, it just…feels like we have a lot to make up for, ya know?"

He smiles and kisses the tip of my nose as he looks down at me.

"I know," he whispers, and a veil of sadness falls over his eyes. I swallow as I realize that the time we have left could very well be limited.

He kisses me one more time then slides off the bed.

"Do you want to come over for dinner tonight?" he asks. "I know Annabelle would love it if you did."

I smile and nod.

"Of course," I say. "I miss her."

He smiles.

"You have no idea how amazing it is to hear you talk about her like that," he says. I smile back. "I'll see you tonight."

I GET DRESSED and go for a walk down the street, waving to people who are packing up their cars to head back home for the school year.

I remember that feeling—like something beautiful was coming to an end. The inevitable sunset on a perfect summer. Especially the summers I spent with him—those were always a little harder to say goodbye to than any summer before.

I'm supposed to be off today, but after a few more hours of trying to keep myself busy, I decide to head to the store. I'm sure they could use the help—it's the last weekend before schools start again, and things are nuts in Meade Lake right now. When I come through the back door, Derrick is at the front desk, leaning across it to point to a map that a young man is holding.

"This here is Deep Water Point," he says, pointing to

a spot at the top of the map. "This end of the lake is where most of the restaurants and the resort are."

"Great, thanks," the man says, folding it up and heading out the door. Derrick grabs a few hangers from behind the counter and walks them around the front, sticking them on one of the clothing racks.

"Hey," I say, startling him.

"Hey," he says with his classic smile, "what are you doing here?"

I shrug.

"Not much to do on my day off," I say, catching a glimpse of Ryder out the window, making his way up from the docks with a water tube under each of his perfectly sculpted arms.

"Mhmm," Derrick says. "Sure it's not 'cause you've had a, uh, change of heart?" He elbows me playfully, and I realize that I've been made. I'm totally drooling over Ryder, and I'm not even hiding it. I shove him back with a smile, but there's really no use in denying it.

Derrick chuckles to himself.

"What?" I ask.

"Nothin'," he says. "Just that, when we were kids, how you two are now is sort of how I always pictured it. Just weird when that stuff comes true."

I smile at him and tilt my head.

Me too, Derrick. Me too.

"I'm glad you're here, ya know, for his treatments," he says. I swallow and whip my head to him. I forgot about that. Chemo starts this week. I'm about to ask about it when I hear the jingle of the bell above the door.

"Well, aren't you a sight for sore eyes," he says, laying the tubes down on a pile next to the register and making his way toward me. Without hesitation, he wraps his arms around my waist and pulls me into him, kissing my lips softly but urgently at the same time. Like he wants to be gentle, but he also wants me to know how badly he needs this kiss.

I recognize the feeling because I have the same one.

"Right back to where ya started, aren't ya?" Derrick chuckles as he walks back to the register.

"What are you doing here?" he asks.

"I have some free time, being that you guys are my only friends around here," I say. He laughs and shakes his head. "So I thought I'd come see if you guys need any help."

He smiles.

"I'm about to put some air in these babies and then head back down to the water and wait for the afternoon return. Wanna join?"

I smile. I think we both already know the answer to that.

We help a group of young people get on their jet skis and head out.

We give a family the rundown on how to drive a pontoon and size everyone for their life vests.

I smile to myself as a group of women in their twenties makes eyes in Ryder's direction. One asks him to tighten her life vest and looks less than pleased when I offer instead. Her friend leans over the side of her kayak, letting her breasts press together into a perfect crease.

"You wanna join us?" she asks Ryder over the rims of her sunglasses. He smiles and shakes his head.

"Nah, you ladies don't need an old man like me

holdin' ya back," he says, helping the last one in her kayak.

"You could hold me, alright," one of them mutters, sending the rest of them into a fit of shameless, flirtatious laughter.

"Aww, come on. It's our girl's last outing as a single woman!" another chimes in.

I have to hand it to them, they're ballsy.

He smiles and shakes his head again.

"Thanks, ladies, but I got me a girl I wanna spend the rest of my days on the water with."

He turns to me with a smile, and I feel my insides melt. I don't even notice the girls paddling away, or the wake from the boats, or the traffic above. I only see him.

The rest of my days.

A little while later, we help a middle-aged couple get into their double kayaks. I hold the boat steady while Ryder helps the woman get into hers.

"Thanks, honey," she says to him. Then she nods to her husband in his kayak. "We're here for our thirtieth anniversary."

"Thirty? Wow!" Ryder says with his classic smile.

"That's right. That lady has been crazy enough to put up with my ass for three decades," the man says with a hearty laugh.

"Thirty years is impressive," I say. "What a milestone."

The couple turns to each other, and their faces light up simultaneously.

"When you're with the right one, honey, it doesn't feel impressive. It just feels like it's exactly how it's supposed to be." We smile and give them a shove then wave until they make it out into the open water.

Ryder turns to me, walking toward me and cupping my face in his hands.

"Like it's exactly how it's supposed to be," he whispers before kissing me.

WE FINISH up a few hours later, collecting the last of the jackets and tying up the boats for the night. We say goodnight to Derrick and walk out to the lot.

"You're still coming tonight, right?" he asks.

"Of course. I was just gonna go shower first, get the lake off me," I tell him. He smiles, and his eyes drop to the ground.

"What?" I ask him with a smile.

"Nothin'."

"No, tell me," I urge. He smiles again.

"I just, uh, I guess I'm just picturing you in the shower," he says with a shrug. Then he leans forward, kisses my cheek, and turns and gets in his car. "See you soon."

As he drives off, I shake off his words.

But I don't do a good enough job. Because I get home, get in the shower, and picture *him*.

I choose a halter dress and some sandals and make my way back over to Big Moon Drive. While my heart and my libido have been waiting for Ryder, I'm more anxious to see Annabelle again.

I pull into the gravel driveway and turn off my engine, and before I'm out of the car, the front door opens. Annabelle shoots off the front porch and into my arms.

"Hey, you!" I say, swinging her around. She giggles

ecstatically, and when I stop, she wraps her arms and legs around me and squeezes me tight.

I grab my bag and walk up the front steps, her on my hip. Ryder's leaning against the door jamb with a smile on his face. He takes my bag from my shoulder and holds his hand out to usher us in.

"How are you, honey?" I ask her as I set her down on the floor. She smiles.

"I'm good! Wanna see my new makeup kit? Miss Alma got it for me!" she says, scurrying down the hall to her room before I can answer.

I look to Ryder.

"Makeup already, huh? You're in trouble," I tell him. He smiles.

"I know, I know. Wait till you see the sky-blue eyeshadow. She's a pro at it. I know because I've been trying to wash the remnants of it off my own eyelids for the last two hours," he says. I laugh.

"Well, that's okay," I tell him as I walk toward him, "I think blue is your color."

"Oh, is it?" he asks, reaching a hand out and tugging me toward him. Just as our lips are about to meet, we hear the scurrying of little feet down the hardwood, and I quickly take a step back. He gives me a puzzled look, like he's not sure why I pulled away, then kneels down to catch her in her tracks.

"Daddy! I need to show Mila my makeup!" she says, kicking from over his shoulder. He flips her over his shoulder and tickles her sides, and a shriek of laughter escapes from her.

"After dinner, little one," he says, flipping her back over and walking her out to the deck. He sits her in a chair at the table then pulls out the one across from her for me.

"No, Daddy. Mila sits next to *me*," she says. Ryder's eyes widen as he looks up at me.

"Ouch," he says, feigning heartbreak. "Fine." He pulls out the chair next to her, and I gladly take it.

"Mila, do you like makeup?" she asks me, helping herself to the hot dog that Ryder had all ready for her on her plate. I smile as he hands me the salad bowl and pours some wine in my glass.

"I do on special occasions," I tell her.

"But not all the time?" she asks between bites.

"No, not all the time," I tell her.

"Because she's beautiful without it," Ryder says, smiling at me. I feel the flutters in my stomach that only Ryder Casey has given me in my lifetime.

"She is very beautiful, like Princess Cassidy!" Annabelle says. I give him a puzzled look.

"Princess Cassidy is the character from our current *favorite* bedtime story," he explains. I nod.

"Wow, I am *honored,*" I tell her. She giggles.

We finish up dinner, and I help wash Annabelle up while he brings all the dishes inside. After everything is cleaned up, he tells her it's time for bed.

"Come on, little one. It's late," he says. "Off to your room."

Like an automatic reaction, her bottom lip juts out in the most epic pout I've ever seen.

"I wanna stay up with you and Mila, Daddy," she says. He sticks his lip out to match hers then scoops her up.

"Sorry, kiddo. You're still little. You need your beauty sleep," he says, kissing the tip of her nose.

"I want Mila to put me to bed," she says. My heart rate kicks up in my chest.

Ryder turns to me with big eyes.

"Aww, I don't think Miss Mila wants to—"

"I'd love to," I say, cutting him off. She leans out of his arms and into mine, and I raise my eyebrows at him as we walk down the hall to her room.

I help her pull on her bright-purple flower night-gown and plug in her nightlight. She instructs me on how to turn on her music box, and then we brush her teeth. She tells me which stuffed animal goes on which side of her and which blanket goes on top of which. Then I snuggle in next to her as I pick up *Princess Cassidy*.

We get through the first two pages before I feel the weight of her head on my shoulder. I stealthily sneak out from under her and click off her lamp. I put the book on her nightstand and slink over to the door.

"Mila," she says, and I freeze just as I'm about to shut the door.

"Yes, sweetie?"

"I love you," she says sleepily then rolls over to the other side.

It catches me by surprise, and I smile.

"I love you too, sweetie girl," I say then close the door.

I pause for a moment, resting my head against the oak of her door. I know she's only a child, and I know a child can't fathom what it means to *really* love someone.

Can they?

I mean, kids only know to say exactly what they're feeling. How beautifully honest they are.

I walk back down the hallway and see Ryder lying on the couch. He mutes the television and sits up.

"Hey," he says, "how did it go?"

"Mission accomplished," I tell him, plopping down on the couch beside him and tucking my legs up underneath me.

"I have to admit," he says, reaching his hand across and rubbing my thigh. "I'm a little jealous. In her whole life, I have never been second to anyone."

I smile and take his hand.

"But I guess if I have to take second place, I'm glad it's to you," he says. I scoot in next to him.

"She told me she loves me," I say, looking down at our intertwined hands. I chuckle. "I guess I shouldn't let it go to my head, though, huh?"

He reaches a hand up and tucks a piece of hair behind my ear. He leans forward and kisses me so softly that it makes me desperate for more.

"She did, huh?" he asks. I nod. "She's not the only one."

He pulls me on top of him so that I'm straddling him on the couch. I let my tongue slide into his mouth and massage his, and then I can feel what I'm doing to him through his jeans. I let myself grind against him lightly at first, but as his kisses get more fiery, more intense, I can't help but move faster. When his hand slides up my leg and under my dress, I grab it.

"What if she wakes up?" I ask him. He sighs and presses his forehead to mine.

"I guess we could take this to my bedroom—where there's a door that locks," he says with a mischievous smile.

He pushes up and scoots to the edge of the couch, me still on his lap.

"Stay the night," he whispers, kissing my neck softly.

"No," I whisper back.

"Mila, stay with me," he says again. I shake my head as he nibbles at my ear and shoulder.

"No."

"Why?"

"What will she think when she wakes up and I'm still here?" I ask him. But what I'm really asking is, how can I let her get attached? What if this doesn't work again? What if treatment doesn't...what if everything will be different in a year?

This makes him pause.

"Is that what you're worried about?"

No.

I nod.

"Yes," I say.

He pulls me in closer.

"Mila, I have absolutely no idea what the rest of my life looks like at this point," he says, "but I know that I want you to be a part of it."

My stomach flips. He intertwines our fingers again and looks down at them.

"If my time really is...limited," he says, pausing, I think, to gather himself, "I want to show my daughter how she should be loved. I want her to see how important it is to spend her time with the people she loves. And that she shouldn't take any of it for granted."

I don't even realize I'm crying until the tears fall from my eyes when I blink.

He leans forward and kisses me again, grinding himself back against me. I tighten my thighs around his body, pulling him into me as close as possible. He pushes to his feet and grips my ass, carrying me down the hallway to his room. He closes the door quietly and brings me to his bed. He slides his hands up underneath my dress, and I buck my hips toward him.

He hooks his thumbs around my panties and pulls them down my legs. He pushes my knees apart and slowly slides his hand back up until he finds my spot. He circles it as he reaches his other hand up and unties the halter. He lets it fall and reaches up to run his hands over my breasts, hardening them with just his touch. Suddenly, my entire body aches for him. I press his hand into my chest, and my other hand is on top of his between my legs.

"Easy, baby," he says, "we're getting there."

But I hardly hear him. I buck my hips at him again.

"Ryder, we're twelve years overdue for this," I tell him. "Don't make me wait anymore."

He smiles then reaches up to pull his t-shirt over his head.

I reach up to unbuckle his belt and tug his jeans and boxers down then fall back on the bed and spread my legs wider than before. He crawls up the bed so that he's hovering over me, and I pull him down for a long kiss.

"I need you," I tell him when we finally come up for air. He presses his forehead to mine.

"For as long as I'm alive," he tells me. I pull myself up and flip him over onto the bed. I crawl up him, leaving kisses from his hips up to his chest then to his lips.

Our eyes lock, and I lower myself onto him slowly. He presses his head back into his pillow and squeezes my hips.

"Oh, God, Mila," he groans as I begin to move. He reaches his hands up and grabs onto my breasts, squeezing them, making me lose my mind with every tantalizing pinch. I can feel my wetness on him now, and I'm losing control of my body. He pushes himself up, pulling me in for a long, hard kiss, then flips me over onto my back. He pulls my leg up over his shoulder and kisses it then pushes into me harder, deeper, until I'm biting down on my lip to keep from making too much noise. He moves once more, in sync with his hand on my outside, and I explode.

Aftershocks roll through my body as he kisses me, hard then soft. He collapses next to me, draping his arms over me and pulling me into him.

We lie like that for a while, staring out at the lake through the sliding glass door in his room.

I trace the veins in his arms as I listen to his breathing, slow and steady, like the soft ripples on the water in front of us.

"Ryder?" I whisper.

"Hmm?"

"Tell me about Maura," I whisper, biting my lip. I want to know more. I want to know about the woman who brought this beautiful man to life. Who *gave* life to Annabelle. He swallows.

"What do you want to know?" he asks.

"Everything," I say.

"Mmm," he says, propping his head up. "She was like the sun. Everything pointed to her, revolved around her, but she gave it no mind. She just lit everyone and everything else up. She wanted everyone to shine."

I smile.

"She was so level-headed and forgiving," he goes on. "She reminded me that living isn't just waiting to die."

I swallow.

"Was she...was she your soulmate?"

He rolls me over so we're nose to nose and tucks an arm under my pillow.

"If I'm being honest, I don't know if I really believe in all that," he tells me. "But if I did, as much as I loved her, I think I'd have to say no."

My eyes widen.

"In all my life, there has been one love that's completely rocked me. And that was you. Our love was good, bad, and the absolute ugliest, and I'd do every second of it over again—every single moment—if it meant that I'd end up back here, with you, in this bed."

23

It's been a few days since I spent the night at Ryder's. The next morning was as normal as ever. We were up before Annabelle, and I had pancakes and bacon waiting for her when she woke up. She didn't think anything of it, didn't even blink. And when Ryder kissed my cheek in front of her, she smiled and kissed my other cheek.

But I still need boundaries. If not for her, than for me. Because what if Ryder...what if things are different in a year? Or less? What if I can't be around or see her as much? If I get too attached, it'll destroy me all over again.

I'm back at the shop, and I have knots in my stomach. Ryder went in for his first round of treatment this morning, but I stayed back to help Derrick close up the summer stuff and get ready for the winter shipments. Alma has Annabelle, and I'm trying to make things as smooth and easy for everyone else as possible.

Derrick and I walk across the street to pull the last of the boats up for the season when we see Ryder down below, chaining them up to the trailer. His face is hard and serious, his biceps flexed as he hoists the weight of the boats up. We watch as he walks down the dock to lock up the shed.

"What is he doing here?" I ask. Derrick sighs as he looks down the hill at his friend.

"Last time, the effects didn't kick in till a few days later," Derrick says. "He's probably just trying to get in as much as he can."

I nod and swallow.

He doesn't *look* sick. He looks...fucking beautiful. He's big and strong and brooding, but at the same time, so full of light.

I think about what he said about Maura—that she was his sun. And I think that's what I feel about him. He lights up every part of my life, including the ones that have been dark for more than a decade.

"Should we help him?" I ask. Derrick shakes his head.

"I think he needs this. He needs to know he's still helping."

I nod and follow Derrick back inside. He finishes putting away the last of the summer gear and tells me he's heading out. I stay back to unpack some of the boxes in the storage room so that it's easier to stock the winter racks tomorrow.

As I'm standing on my tiptoes to reach one of the big boxes from the back of the room, I hear the creak of the door behind me. Ryder steps in, and I freeze.

The look on his face is still so hard as he narrows his eyes on me. He's carrying a box, and he lowers it down slowly to the ground, his eyes never falling from mine.

I want to ask him how he feels, what it was like, if

he's scared. I want to ask him what the doctors said today or if he needs anything.

But he stalks toward me with such presence, such determination, that I can't find any words. Instead, he reaches for my hips and pulls me into him, letting his tongue find mine with such hunger that it makes me gasp. Our lips crash into each other, and his hands are searching my body underneath my shirt.

"Let's go home," he tells me, and I nod.

When we get back to his house, we take a long, hot shower together. He washes my hair and my back, and I return the favor. There's something so sensual about being in here with him, the air around us thick and hot, our bodies wet and rubbing against each other. I look up at him as he rinses his hair. I want to ask him if he's okay. Then, in a moment's time, his lips crash into mine again, and I realize that with the insatiable mode in which he is kissing me, he's answering my question. He's not okay, and he needs me. Right now. Just like this. So, I give him whatever he needs. However he needs to stay afloat, that's what I'll be for him.

He pushes me back gently against the tile wall of the shower and lifts me up so that my legs can wrap around his waist. He thrusts his tongue into my mouth, hoisting me up with one arm. And within a mere moment, he's inside of me, my back flat against the cold wall as he thrusts in and out, harder and harder.

If nothing else were happening, it would probably be hottest sex I've ever had.

Okay, to be fair, cancer and all, it's *still* the hottest sex I've ever had.

But it's so much more than that.

He's holding me so tight to his body, and I'm

clenching myself around him with every muscle in my body.

"Ryder," I whisper, clawing at his back as he pushes up against me.

He moans, and I squeeze myself around him, making him drop his head back.

I kiss and lick and nip his neck, and it pushes him over the edge.

He hoists me up a little more with one arm, and the change of angle drives me wild. He smacks his other hand against the wall behind me with one more hard thrust.

"Fuck," he groans, dropping his head to mine. I wrap my hands around his neck and pull him into me, letting him catch his breath. He kisses the top of my head and slowly slides out of me, lowering me to the ground.

After we catch our breath, we rinse back off, get dressed, and slip under the covers of his bed.

We still haven't spoken, but he wraps his arms around me. I look at the clock. It's only seven o'clock.

"I was going to take Annabelle out for a dinner date tonight," he says. "Take advantage of feeling good while I still do. Will you join us?"

I smile and tilt my head.

"You two should go," I say. "She deserves some time alone with you."

He thinks for a moment then nods. He reaches down and pulls my hand to his lips.

"I'll see you tomorrow?" he asks. I nod.

"I'll be around," I tell him with a smile. He kisses me once more then lies back down next to me.

"Just a few more minutes," he whispers.

. . .

As I GET in my car and stare out at the sun dipping down behind the black mountains, the tears fall, pouring from my eyes like waterfalls.

My Ryder is going to get sick soon, and I could be running out of time.

24

I get home that night and begin making as many freezer meals as physically possible before running out of freezer space. Pasta sauce, pot roast, Italian chicken, soup. Anything I can do to make their lives easier.

And then I lie down in bed, slipping into the deepest sleep I've had in a long time.

I WAKE up before the sun, and I still have a few hours before the shop opens. My stomach is turning, my vision tunneling as I stare up at the ceiling. The oak fan blades spin a million miles a minute, sending me into a loop of fear, wondering how the chemicals they're going to pump into his body will affect him. If they'll strip him of anything familiar, take away everything that's mine.

I hop up and dig through my bag for my sneakers. I grab a sports bra and a pair of shorts and walk out the front door.

I actually don't like running; I have a long history of

despising physical activity. But this crazy energy that's brewing inside me needs to be let out. I run down the street and come to a fork. One side is wooded with a few sparse houses. The other is clear-blue water melding into the dark-green mountains in the background. I turn toward the water and push up the hill in front of me, homing in on the lake. If I just keep pushing through the trees, up the hill…if I keep moving, I'll reach it. The clear blue, the big, lapping wakes that hold all the answers I'm looking for.

At least, it used to.

Until it took all the answers away.

But it's still so clear, so blue, so big and sure of itself.

I can feel the burn in my hamstrings and my lungs as I reach the crest of the hill, when I hear breathing from up ahead. I narrow my eyes at a clearing in the trees, and I see him, flying down the road with such anger in every step that it feels like the earth beneath my feet is rattling.

"Derrick?" I call out, and his eyes lift from the road to me. He's huffing and puffing, sweat pouring down his brow. He comes to a halt a few feet from me, wiping his temple on his arm.

"Hey," he says.

I come to a stop, too, more than happy to have an excuse for a walk-break less than two miles into my run.

He looks down at the ground again, kicking a small pebble in front of him. Then he looks up to me. I plead to him with my eyes, begging him to tell me something good. Begging him to let me know that everything is going to be okay. That our boy is going to be fine. That there will be a lot more cookouts and bedtime stories. More tomorrows.

He looks down at me, and I can see something building up in his eyes. I know what it is because I have the same thing in my heart.

He opens his mouth like he's going to say something then closes it again. He puts his hand on my shoulder, then the other one.

Then he lets go, steps around me, and keeps going.

I look out over the water, shades of black and blue and green, and let a tear roll down my cheek.

My shift is supposed to start at lunch, but looking at the clock and watching the minutes roll by is killing me. I want to be with him today. To see him, make sure with my own two eyes that he's okay. But he made me promise not to ditch the shop today. Told me Derrick needed me more and that he would be fine.

I head in a little earlier and put my car in park in the lot. It's quieter now that it's in between seasons, but Derrick and I have a lot of winterizing to do today— putting away tubes and water skis, pulling down snowboards and actual skis.

I walk across the lot, gazing out at the lake, when I catch a glimpse of him, the most beautiful man in the world, out on the docks. He's pulling up the poles at the end of the dock that keep it steady in the water.

I can still see his muscles bulging, his eyes calm, no strain in his face, no evidence of all his body has just endured. I walk down the steps and stand at the edge of the dock, watching him in silence for a few seconds. Everything is so normal, and I want to bask in it before it disappears altogether.

"Well, aren't you a sight for sore eyes," he says when

he finally notices me. I'm getting used to this greeting. I give him a pained smile, wrapping my arms around myself.

"What are you doing here?" I ask. "Shouldn't you be resting?"

He lays one of the poles down on the ground as he makes his way down the dock toward me. His lips pull up into a smile, and he pushes a piece of hair out of my face. He lets his fingers trace my chin, my lips. His other hand cups my cheek, and he strokes it with his thumb. I watch as his eyes scan my face, paying close attention to every detail, lingering on every corner. He pulls me in for a kiss, one so soft I'm sure it could kill me.

"I feel like I could walk on water," he whispers then kisses me again. I close my eyes and let him hold me like this for a moment before I snap back to reality. To the cancer.

"Seriously, though, shouldn't you get home?"

He chuckles.

"No, baby," he whispers, and chills ripple across my skin. It's been so long since he's called me that. "I'm okay for now. So let's just keep on goin'."

Derrick and Ryder go through the day like nothing else is going on in their lives. Laughing and joking, moving all the summer displays to the back, replacing all the kayaks with snow tubes and toboggans.

Toward the end of the day, Derrick closes up in the back and heads out to cover Ryder's shift at Lou's. It's the last one for a while because Lou, and Ryder, and Derrick—and seemingly everyone—knows that he won't be up to it soon. That he won't be able to work *one* job, let alone two. It's like everyone around us is bracing themselves.

I help the last customers of the day find jackets and ski goggles and then send them to the front so that Ryder can check them out. I lean up against the door jamb of the storage room and watch as he smiles at them, listen as he suggests Brenda's Pizza for dinner, and tells them that the Lakeside Creamery is still open for another week or so before they close for the winter.

"You guys will love it here," he tells them, and then his eyes meet mine from across the room. "It's the best place in the world to be with the person you love."

I smile back at him and tuck away into the storage room, digging through boxes to find some more sweat-shirts to hang on the racks at the front of the room. After a few minutes, I hear the ding of the bell above the door. I hear Ryder click the lock, and I hear him clicking on the mouse to close down the computer.

I picture him—even though he's just feet away from me in the other room—smiling. Talking to the customers. The way he raised his eyebrows at me when he spoke. I picture that crooked smile, and I want to taste it. I picture his long hands that have years of work etched in them but are still the gentlest hands to ever have touched me.

And I realize that I miss him, even though he's a room away.

And it's terrifying to me how much I've grown to want him around, like everything I felt for him at sixteen, seventeen, eighteen...has been amplified. Like my heart went ahead and made a decision to love him harder, longer, more intensely than I knew was possible. It betrayed me; it didn't give me a moment, an option, to protect myself. I'm all in again.

"If I could end all my work days watching you bend

over to unload these boxes, I'd be one happy son of a bitch," he says, posting up against the wall behind me and crossing his arms over his chest. I jump and clutch my chest, not aware that he had come in. I laugh and give him a look.

Then, I turn back around and bend, as controlled as possible, to grab another pile of shirts from the box in front of me. I lift myself back up painfully slow, making sure to stick my ass out just a *tad* more than I had been before I knew he was in here.

I turn back to him slowly. His smile has faded, but his eyes stay locked on me, scanning my body until they reach mine. He takes a step toward me.

"If I could end all my days with you, period, I'd be happy," he says, his voice a low whisper. I swallow. He takes another step toward me, this time nudging the closet door shut with his foot. He reaches me and pushes me gently against the wall behind me. He kisses me lightly at first, and then the urgency takes over, his tongue on mine and his hands in my hair. I tug at the hem of his shirt, lifting it up over his head. His chest is broad and sculpted, speckled with a little hair and warm against my body. He reaches down and pulls up mine, letting the fabric drag across my skin as he pulls it up over my head. I reach back and unclasp my bra, letting it trail down off my arms. His eyes alight as he stares at me, his hands sliding up my thighs until they reach my breasts, squeezing and caressing them until I'm hard under his touch.

He scoops me up with one arm and uses his other hand to unbutton my jeans. I help him tug them down over my hips and shimmy free from them then wrap my legs around his waist.

He sets me back down on the floor and tugs at my panties till they fall to the floor. I return the favor, and his pants and boxers lie in a heap next to mine. I take in the sight of every inch of him, wanting to both admire and devour him at the same time. I feel that magnetic pull toward him, like my body needs him within a certain distance. He drops to his knees for a moment in front of me, gently guiding me back to the wall, like he knows I'll need the support. He brings his mouth to my center, and I feel my legs wobble instantly. I drop my head back against the wall and run my fingers through his hair, and he makes love to me with his mouth. Then, he stands back up, grabbing my hips with both hands and lifting me back up to him. I feel his hard length against me as I slide up his body, locking myself around him. He kisses me hard, his tongue tracing mine, and then lifts me off for a moment. He looks into my eyes with this intensity that makes my blood run cold and then slowly guides himself inside of me. We both moan together, and I wrap my arms around his neck, holding him as close to me as possible, savoring the very moment that our bodies become one. He begins to move in and out, and I'm swimming in that same glorious unknown territory that still feels so familiar. I clench myself around him, making every stroke in and out an insane ride.

"Ryder," I moan, and it makes his grip on me grow tighter. I dig my nails into his skin as his hands slide up my ass and grab hold of my shoulders, holding me in place. He switches up the angle, and I grow louder.

"*Ryder,*" I say in a throaty voice, as both a warning and a cry for more.

"Oh, baby," he whispers into my hair before he

carries me across the closet to a small table we use for folding in the back corner. He shoves everything off of it, crashing to the floor, then lays me down gently. He slides out of me, leaving me silently screaming for him to come back. His lips trail up my body, over my stomach, and he takes each of my breasts into his mouth for just a long enough moment to make me pant, my hips bucking in his direction.

"*Ryder,*" I say again, "come *on.*"

He smiles as he looks down at me, and I watch as his eyes move across my face. He's studying me like he's trying to memorize every corner of my face, and then I realize, that's *exactly* what he's doing.

Making love to me like it's the last time.

Before I can dwell on the moment, though, he's back inside of me just as he takes my mouth in his, crashing into me from every direction and making my head spin.

He pounds in, slowly out, and back in again, and I'm arching my back to savor the way he hits a spot that I had long since written off as imaginary.

"God damn, Mila," he groans just before one last long stroke. And then he freezes above me. When he catches his breath, he bends down to kiss my lips and trace my jaw with his thumb.

"Cosmic," I whisper. He looks at me quizzically, then a smile appears on his lips.

"What?" he asks. I reach up and run my fingers through his hair.

"You and me. We're cosmic." Because that's just what we are. Two people that don't make a lot of sense, but the universe made a decision about us that cannot be fought. He bends down and kisses me once more.

"Cosmic," he says.

. . .

WHEN WE LEAVE THE SHOP, we pick up Annabelle from Alma's and grab a pizza from Brenda's for a late-night dinner. The three of us eat it over the island in the kitchen, laughing as she tells us about her day. She's such a bright little girl, so much knowledge in her little head. It's like, even though she's too young to remember her mother, she absorbed all her smarts, soaked in all her goodness, all the saint like qualities that I've heard so much about. They're reincarnated in her, and sometimes, it's hard to remember she's a child.

But then she rubs her eyes with the back of her little hand, a big yawn escaping her little body. I help wipe her hands and mouth with a wet paper towel and tap her nose with my finger.

"I love you, Mila," she says as she looks up at me, her big eyes boring holes into me. I feel Ryder's eyes on me as he swallows, but my gaze never wavers from her.

"I love you too, sweet girl," I say, kissing her forehead.

"I wish you could stay with us here at our house," she says. Ryder clears his throat next to me, but I ignore it. I scoop her up, and she wraps her arms around my neck.

"Let's get you to bed," I whisper. She nods and rests her chin on my shoulder. I change her into her nightgown and help her brush her teeth. She chooses *I'll Love You Forever* tonight, and then she sinks into her pile of pink and purple pillows and blankets and is out in a blink. I brush the hair from her face and kiss her head one more time.

"Goodnight, my sweet girl," I whisper. "I love you."

· · ·

WHEN I GET BACK out to the living room, he's waiting for me on the couch.

"See," he says, a smug look on his face. "I'm not the only one who wants you to stay." I roll my eyes at him as I scoot closer to him and nestle into the crook of his arm. He wraps it around me, the glow of the television the only light. I look up at him and study the lines on his face like I'm connecting the dots.

"You just gonna keep staring at me, or what?" he asks with a smile without moving his eyes from the T.V. I smile.

"Sorry," I whisper, but to my own surprise, my voice cracks. He turns to look at me just as the first tear rolls down my cheek. He pushes himself up and turns to me, pulling me into him closer.

"Baby?" he says. "Hey, what's the matter?"

And when he does that, when he calls me baby like he used to, it's like something has crashed into the damn floodgates.

He turns to me completely, using his thumbs to swipe away my tears. He cups my face and kisses my forehead until I gather myself.

"I cannot lose you," I finally manage to whisper. I watch his Adam's apple bob as he swallows. "Not when I finally have you again. I can't."

I hate myself for making this about me. I hate myself for letting myself break in front of him. But Ryder does just what he always has. He pulls me into him, tucking me into him like only he knows how, wrapping his arms around me and clutching my head to his chest.

"Hey," he says, "hey, shh."

I finally gather myself and take the chance of looking up at him. He kisses me so softly that it feels like our lips barely touch.

I wait for him to tell me he's okay, he's not going anywhere. That he won't leave me again. But he doesn't, because he won't lie to me. He won't promise not to hurt me again, because he'd never break a promise to me.

Instead, he pulls me in for another kiss, this time hard and longing and intense. I pull myself up onto my knees and straddle him on the couch, running my fingers through his hair.

His hands slide up my back and under my shirt, sending an electric current through my whole body. I feel him unclasp my bra, and I jump back, despite every fiber of my being pulling me toward him, begging for more.

"Are you sure?" I ask him. "I don't want to do too much. I don't want you to overdo it."

He leans up to kiss me. When he pulls back, I see his eyes are glassy with tears that haven't fallen yet, and I feel like my heart is made of glass.

"Let me make love to you like you deserve," he says. "Before…" His voice trails off, and I hold my breath. "This could be it, for a while."

I nod and pull him into me, letting him carry me back to his room, letting him whittle away at another piece of me that I know he'll take forever.

25

The next morning, I pull up to the shop and get out, pulling my fleece around me tighter. I forgot how quickly winter descends on this place, like there's a sharp line drawn on the calendar where the temperature has to drop. I pull my hair out from my collar and tie it up in a bun.

I stroll through the glass doors with a smile on my face, memories of last night on my mind and still on my skin in places no one else will see. I can't wait to see him today. I can't wait to steal glances at him while he helps people try on ski goggles, gives them directions to the slopes, tells them they have to stop at Lou's for a burger.

But when I walk through the door, I see chaos.

There's a long line of people already at the register, lining up for their supplies and coats and gloves before the slopes open.

Derrick's running—literally—from behind the counter to different racks, grabbing things for people, pointing to other spots in the store for other customers, then running back to ring people up. I scurry behind the counter, taking over for him just as he looks like his head is about to explode.

"Thank God," he says as he scoots back out to help more people on the floor.

I scan people out, point to the slope maps, and repeat the hours of the slopes and tubing courses what feels like four million times. Then, finally, I check the last person out. The bell on the door rings as I wave good-bye, then Derrick emerges from the back of the store and plasters his hands on the counter in front of me. He takes in a long breath then finally looks up at me.

"Nothing like ski season to get the blood flowing," he says with a forced smile. I swallow and nod.

"Where is he?" I ask. He takes in another long breath and swipes a hand down his face.

"It, uh…it kicked in, late last night," he says. "He's been puking since three o'clock this morning."

My heart's rattling in my chest, banging against the inside of my ribcage.

"Is it…is it supposed to happen that fast? Is it—"

"Mama says it can change from patient to patient, cancer to cancer," Derrick says. He looks around the store. "Mama has Annabelle today so that he can rest. Now that the morning rush is over, I can call Teddy and have him come in for the lunch crowd. You can go to him," he says. I draw in a long, shuddered breath then nod. He reaches out for my hand, and I take it reluctantly. He squeezes it for a moment, and I realize that I don't like the look in his eye. The look of uncertainty, like there's no time to waste. He lets go, and I head out to my car.

I stop at the diner for some homemade noodle soup then speed down Lakeside Highway toward Big Moon

Drive. I feel like my tires aren't even touching the ground by the time I reach the cul-de-sac, and I skid to a halt in his driveway. I hop out and barge through the front door, running on adrenaline.

"Ryder?" I call out, dropping my things on the front table and putting the soup in the fridge. I shimmy out of my coat as I look around. "Ryder? Where are you?"

I hear a toilet flush down the hall, and I make my way through his bedroom.

"Ryder?" I ask, reaching for the bathroom door.

"Don't come in here," he says, his voice hoarse and scratchy.

"Why? Are you alright?" I ask.

"Just don't come in," he says. "You don't need to see—"

I push the door open and see him on the ground, wrapped around the toilet, his face buried in the crook of his arm. His brow is wet with sweat, and his eyes are sunken in his head with thick purple bags beneath them.

"Oh, Ryder," I whisper, kneeling down.

"No," he whispers back. "Go."

But I ignore him.

I grab a washcloth from the towel rack and run it under cold water. I help him sit back and dab it across his forehead. I run it down his neck then press it to his cheeks. When a little bit of the color is restored in his face, I ask him if he thinks he can stand. He nods and grabs hold of the tub, and I take hold of his other hand. As his weight crushes down on me, it takes every muscle in my body to keep him up. We walk the few steps to his bed, and I pull the covers down as he crashes down onto it.

I strip off his sweat-soaked t-shirt and prop him up

on all the pillows on his bed. I stand on the bed to turn his fan on and then hop down. I push the hair off of his face and stare down at him, still as beautiful and perfect as ever.

While he sleeps, I slip off to the kitchen, making some tea and honey. I do a load of Annabelle's laundry and make her bed. I sweep, mop, and dust the entire first floor. I make more freezer meals and unload the dishwasher.

I heat up the soup and bring it back to his room. He stirs gently when he hears the creak of the door, and his eyes open slowly. A pained smile tugs at his lips.

"Hey," he says, closing his eyes again. "You're still here."

"Of course," I say, setting the soup down on his side table and sitting next to him on the bed. He reaches a hand up and takes mine. "I brought you some soup from the diner."

He smiles.

"That's about the only thing I could stomach right now," he says. I help him sit up and put the bowl on a tray in front of him. He eats it painfully slow, but I swear, I can see more color in his cheeks with every bite. I watch him eat like it's the most beautiful sight I've ever seen.

"Mm," he says, pushing the tray away when he's eaten all he can handle. "Don't you need to get back to the store?"

I scoff and pull my feet up onto the bed.

"Are you kidding me? I'm not leaving you," I tell him. He smiles and lifts my hand to his lips.

"I'll be fine," he says. "Seriously. Sleep is the best

thing for me when I feel like this. Derrick needs help. Season opens today. It's probably a madhouse."

I smile and wrap my hand around his.

"You're sure you're just going to sleep?" I ask. He nods.

"Go," he says. "I'll be okay. The store must go on!" He holds his hand up dramatically, and I laugh.

"Okay," I whisper, crawling toward him to kiss his head. But to my surprise, he pulls me down so that our lips crash into each other. As I walk toward the door, he calls my name.

"Come back tonight?" he asks. I smile and nod.

"I'll swing by Alma's and grab Annabelle on my way home," I tell him. "And then I'll come check on you."

He smiles and nods.

"And after you do," he says, "don't leave."

I smile, feeling those tears burning at the backs of my eyes again.

I nod as I soak in one last look at him.

THE REST of the afternoon at the store goes by slower than I can handle. As the light is disappearing from the sky, the last of the day's skiers roll in to return their rentals.

"Hey, Derrick," one guy calls out from the last group of the day.

"Hey, guys," Derrick calls from the back of the store. "Good day on the mountain?"

"Always," the guy says again. He's followed by two other guys and three women who are all boasting rosy, snow-bitten cheeks.

"Hi, there," one of the women says as she lays her goggles down on the counter.

"Hi," I say back in a way warmer tone than I'm actually feeling. As I'm collecting their gear, I can feel her eyes on me. Our eyes meet, and she smiles at me.

"You're Ryder's girlfriend, right?" she asks. The question catches me off guard. I haven't been asked that question in over a decade. I smile.

"Um, yeah," I say, basking in how good it feels to fill that role again.

"I'm Jamie. We all went to school with Ryder and Derrick," she says. I nod.

"Ah, nice to meet you," I say.

"How's he feelin'?" one of the guys with her asks. I swallow. I plaster a smile to my face.

"He's hangin' in there," I say. "As tough as ever."

"Sounds about right," Jamie says with a warm smile. They finish turning everything else in. As Derrick and I are putting everything back, I hear Jamie talking on her way out.

"Gosh, I hope he beats it again this time," she says. "That poor little girl already doesn't have a mother. I can't even imagine."

She thinks she's quiet. But she's not.

Derrick's eyes meet mine, and then he clears his throat and disappears into the back.

Since I've been back in Meade Lake, Derrick's played the role of my conscience, my North Star. He's guided me, explained things that were dark and confusing. But he can't explain this. He can't tell me why the best person that we both know is facing a death sentence for the second time in his life. And I know that, through it all, he's hurting, too. He can't be my shoulder through this. Not when he needs a shoulder, too.

I finish at the counter and close up. I grab my coat and scarf and walk outside, letting the freezing air sting my lungs. And then the tears come again, like they've been doing every day for the last week or so.

Only, this time, I can't get them to stop. This sinking, heavy feeling of hopelessness that I've been fending off for a week has finally settled around me, and I don't know how to clear it. I don't know how to keep going. I don't know what I'm supposed to do to keep moving forward, keep living life like it's supposed to be lived, when he's bedridden, taking in a manmade poison to kill the natural poison inside of him.

My shaky hand pulls my phone from my pocket as I scroll through my contacts.

"Mom?" I say when she answers.

TWO HOURS LATER, I'm sitting on the front porch of our lake house when I finally hear the tires across the gravel. I look up and see my mom parking her black Mercedes in the driveway. It's not until I lay eyes on her that I realize how badly I've missed her. Only a few hours apart, yet I haven't made time to go home at all over the last few months and visit. And I didn't realize until right this moment how much that was weighing on my heart.

She walks around to the front of the car and looks up at me for a moment. And when the tears come again, she runs to me, wraps her arms around me, and leads me inside. We sit on the couch, and I cry on her shoulder for what feels like hours.

She strokes my hair and rocks me back and forth in only the way a mother can.

"So, tell me. You fell in love with him again, huh?" she says after a long silence. I wipe the last tears from my cheeks before I turn to her. I press my lips together to stifle a smile. She smiles and brushes my hair behind my shoulder.

"So, it's bad?" she asks. I nod.

"I think so," I tell her. "It's so crazy. I came here trying to find a way to forgive him. I came here with the intent of not *hating* him. And now, I don't think I could stop loving him if I tried. I want to spend every waking minute with him. But now I'm running out of them, and I don't know how—"

The sobs take over again, and she pulls me back into her.

"I know your history was a little...complicated," Mom says. "But sometimes people deserve a second chance. Sometimes."

I swallow. *Like my father.*

"Ryder was always so good to you," she goes on. "And when he came to apologize to your father and me a few years ago, and he asked about you, I could see how much pain your name brought to his eyes. Your story definitely wasn't over. And it still isn't."

I reach up to wipe my nose on my sleeve.

"But I'm running out of time with him," I say. "I wasted all these years staying as far away from him as I could, and now it's too late."

Mom pulls me back into her.

"You don't know that, hon," she says. "You said so yourself; he just started treatment. The doctors still have to evaluate him."

I shake my head.

"Things are already different. He's getting weaker. He can't take care of Annabelle," I say.

"Annabelle?" she asks. I swallow. I realize I didn't mention her to my mom when I called.

"His daughter. She's four. You'd love her, Mom," I say. "She's the most perfect little girl."

Mom stares back at me, a soft smile on her lips.

"A daughter," she whispers. We lean back on the couch and look up at the vaulted ceiling for a little bit, both collecting our thoughts.

"Wow," she whispers as she looks around. I realize she hasn't set foot back in here since Chase died. My dad came back a few times to arrange the rentals, but everything else has been done through his rental company. "I forgot how much I loved this place."

I nod.

"It's been a great home while I came and tried to get my shit together," I say. Then a sad chuckle escapes my lips. "I guess I just got myself into *more* shit, though."

She squeezes my hand.

"Nah, hon. You just got yourself into love. Which can feel just as hard and just as messy. Believe me."

She swallows, and her eyes grow wide. I look at her, and we stare at each other for a moment. I feel like this is it. This is the moment of truth.

"Mom," I say just above a whisper. She swallows again, and I can see the fear building in her eyes. "I think I know what...what Dad did."

She doesn't say anything, just looks down at the gigantic diamond on her ring finger that appeared shortly after I heard the argument over the affair. It replaced her original engagement ring, and when

T. D. COLBERT

someone had asked Mom about it at a party, my dad kissed her cheek and said it was a "symbol of new beginnings."

"I was afraid of that," she whispers. I take her hand in mine. "How long have you known?"

"Since it happened," I say. Her eyes dart to mine. I swallow. "I heard the argument you guys had—I guess when you caught him."

Her eyes are wide.

"Did Chase know?"

"No."

"Why didn't you...why didn't you ever tell me?" she asks.

I shrug.

"I guess I just figured if you wanted me to know, you'd tell me," I say. "And I didn't want you to worry about me thinking less of you for staying."

She cocks her head to one side.

"Do you? Do you think less of me?" she asks.

I look down at my hands.

"I used to," I admit. Her eyebrows jump. "I used to think it made you a little…"

"Weak," she interjects, finishing my exact thought. I nod.

"But now, after coming here…" I say, a knot forming in my throat. "I realize it actually made you stronger. I realize that you made a choice for yourself, and for us, for our family. For Dad."

She swallows back her own tears now, but one escapes. She catches it on her finger and looks up at me.

"I love that man," she whispers. "But I also hated him. For a long, long time. And then I resented everything about him. Especially his job. And I worried so much about you, because I didn't want you to end up like me. In the background of someone else's story. I didn't want that bright light of yours to be dimmed because someone else was always just a *little* bit brighter."

A sad smile appears on her lips as she looks down at our intertwined hands.

"Mom," I say. She looks up at me. "You're the brightest light I've ever known."

She kisses my cheek and strokes it with her thumb.

"My daughter, you are much stronger than you give yourself credit for," she says. "You can do this. Loves like this don't always come around but every decade." She winks. "You can *do* this. And so can he. I'm a call away if you need me, baby."

26

Over the next three weeks, I'm a woman on a mission, moving on autopilot. I'm pulling double-time at the shop with Derrick and picking up Annabelle after work. I bring her home, make dinner for her and Ryder, give her a bath, and get her in bed. I take Ryder to his appointments, sit with him while they pump him full of the "better" poison, then sit with him for the next few days while parts of him are eaten away.

And every time, a piece of me goes right along with it.

It's Sunday, and Derrick sends me home from the shop.

"My mom and sister are taking Annabelle shopping today," he tells me. "The store is slow this morning. Go be with him."

I look at him and smile.

It's actually been weeks since we've just...*been*. All my interactions with Ryder over the last few weeks have been in the form of caretaking. All I've done is make sure he's comfortable and has everything he needs.

I know why Derrick's doing this, and it's not for Ryder.

It's for me.

I don't think twice. I just get in my car and drive to Big Moon Drive.

When I get to the house, I'm surprised to find him up and cooking over the stove. His face lights up when he sees me.

"Hey, you," he says, laying the wooden spoon down on the counter. "What are you doing here?"

"The boss gave me the day off," I say with a smile. "Thought I might like to spend it with my favorite person. Well, *second* favorite person," I say, eyeing a picture of Annabelle on the wall. He laughs and takes my hand.

He kisses my fingertips, then my wrist, then pulls me into him. I wrap my arms around him, and I almost gasp out loud at how much weight he's lost. I guess being with him every day made it hard to see, but feeling his bones sends a chill down my spine. He lifts my chin and kisses my lips, and it gives me the umph I need to keep going.

"How are you feeling?" I ask him when the after-shock of the kiss dies down.

"Much better now," he says with a smile before bending down to kiss me again. I tell him to go sit on the back deck, and I'll bring him the soup when it's done cooking. He grabs a hold of my butt as he shimmies by, and I smile. But before he reaches the end of the island, he stops and clutches a hand to his head.

"What is it?" I ask him. He freezes for a moment then slowly opens his eyes. He shakes his head.

"Just these weird headaches. I think it's the chemo," he tells me. "I'll live."

Will you?

I shake the thought from my head as I continue stirring the chicken soup he started making. I look around at this perfect little house. It's funny how at home I feel here, despite the giant house I can stay in anytime I want across the lake.

But this one feels like him. Feels like home.

Just as I flick the stove off, I hear a crash from the deck. I put the bowls back down on the counter and run to the back door. I find him on his hands and knees. His eyes are wide open, but he's feeling around with his hands.

"Ryder?" I cry. "What happened?"

I kneel down to him and reach for his hands. He jumps when I touch him.

"Ryder? Are you hurt?"

"Mila," he says quietly, "I can't see."

27

I'm looking around the waiting room of the Emergency Room, noticing a lot of random shit. Like the fact that there's one chair that is pushed out from the wall while the others are all lined up against it.

There's a patch on the wall where it looks like something was ripped off, like a poster or something.

There are only two other people here, one an older man who came in with what I assumed to be his daughter, and another man who's holding his hand wrapped in a cloth drenched in blood.

We came by ambulance, and they took Ryder for a brain MRI pretty quickly. So here I am in the waiting room. Just waiting.

I stare across the room at the wall in front of me, studying the patch, when I feel eyes on me. Derrick rushes across the room to me, pulling me to my feet and pulling me into his chest. I wrap my arms around him, but I don't feel anything.

Alma rushes past us, showing her badge at the front desk and going through the doors.

We sit back down slowly, our hands clasped together like we're saying a collective prayer between the two of us.

"So he just...blacked out? Or...what?" Derrick asks after a few moments of silence. I shrug, feeling the tears prickling at the backs of my eyes.

"He fell on the deck. Said he couldn't see," I say. "His vision hadn't come back at all by the time we got here." He nods slowly and sinks back in his chair. Then, he pushes himself back up.

"Hey, are you okay? Ya know...being here?"

I tilt my head and narrow my eyes at him.

Of course I'm not okay.

My boyfriend who has cancer currently can't see. I had to help him to his feet, lead him to the couch, dial 911, and hold his hands as they loaded him up. Tell him it was going to be okay when I didn't know shit.

But then I realize that's not what Derrick means.

He means, am I okay *here*. In this hospital. In the hospital where my brother died.

I suck in a piercing breath and look around.

I hadn't even thought about it. I hadn't even thought about the fact that this is where they pronounced him dead. This is where I told Ryder I wished he had died.

I realize, in this moment, that I didn't think about it, but not because I'm over my brother's death. Not because I've forgotten him. But because being with Ryder brought me the peace I so badly needed all these years.

A sad smile flickers across my lips.

"Yeah," I say, "I'm okay. I just need him to be."

Derrick nods and squeezes my hand.

Alma appears through the big double doors again and calls us through.

"What's going on, Mama?" Derrick asks. "Is he okay?"

"Waiting on MRI results," Alma says, leading us down one long corridor after another. "They're going to admit him in the oncology unit."

I feel that knot start twisting in my stomach again as she leads us up a flight of stairs. After one more long hallway, she stops at one of the doors. She turns to us.

"He's totally petrified, understandably," she says. "We gotta buck up and be strong for him. He needs us, y'all."

We nod and follow her in.

"Hi, baby," she says. "It's me. Derrick's here."

He turns to us, his eyes wide open but looking somewhere on the wall behind us.

"What about—" he starts to say.

"She's here, too," Alma says.

I walk up to the bedside and slowly let my hand take his. He jumps at first then lets his fingers entwine with mine.

"I'm here," I whisper. I reach out and cup his face. "I'm right here."

"And Annabelle?" he asks.

"May has her, baby," Alma says. "Happy as a clam."

AFTER ABOUT AN HOUR, Derrick perks up.

"I'm going to grab something from the cafeteria. What do you all want?"

217

Alma asks for a candy bar; I tell him I'm not hungry. But Ryder asks for a cup of the chicken noodle soup.

"You got it," Derrick says.

He's back within minutes, carrying a *lot* more than a candy bar and some soup. He hands the bar to Alma, plops his own stuff on the table, then goes to hand off the soup to Ryder. And then we all freeze. I take the cup from his hand and grab a spoon. I walk slowly to the bed.

"Here's your soup, Ryder," I tell him. I lean in a little closer as he reaches his hand up to try and find it. "Do you want me to...to feed you?" I whisper.

He lays his head back against his pillow for a moment and closes his eyes.

Then he covers his face with his hands and begins to sob.

Alma takes his other hand; Derrick pats his legs. And we all stand and cry.

A little while later, there's a knock on the door.

A small woman in a white coat walks in. She can't be much taller than five feet. She's got big brown eyes, and her black hair is pulled back into a low bun. Wisps of gray peek out from behind her ears, and there are wrinkles next to her eyes.

"Hello, I'm Dr. Shidu," she says. "I'm a neuro-oncologist here."

"Hello," we all mutter in unison.

"I see you've had a bit of a rough day," she says to Ryder as she walks closer to him. He nods, his eyes moving around, unsure where to land. It breaks my heart each time, like he's lost.

"A bit of a rough few *months*, actually," she says,

correcting herself. "I've reviewed your scans, and I've been in contact with your regular oncologist."

"So, what's going on?" Ryder asks.

Dr. Shidu looks right into his eyes, even though she knows he can't see her. But it's out of respect for him, and I can tell that Ryder can feel it.

"It appears the tumor has grown slightly," she says. "So far, the treatment hasn't had much effect. And it's putting pressure on your optic nerve, which explains the blindness."

I swallow.

Nothing she's said so far makes me feel any better.

"It's worrisome that the treatment hasn't worked thus far," she goes on, "so Dr. Chandler and I would like to schedule you for surgery to try and remove what we can. Following that, you'd go in for more treatment."

We all let it soak in for a minute. Slowly, we nod.

"And if you're able to remove it, and if the treatment works," Alma asks, "his sight…?"

Dr. Shidu takes a breath and nods slowly.

"We're hoping that removing what we can of the tumor will alleviate the pressure," she says, "but there's no guarantee that it hasn't caused permanent damage to the nerve."

"So...are you saying this…" Ryder says, motioning to his eyes, "this could be permanent?"

Dr. Shidu takes a step forward and reaches out for Ryder's hand.

"I'm telling you that we're going to do everything we can. And no matter what happens, there are a lot of resources. But our first goal is to get you cancer-free. In the meantime, we will have you meet with one of our ophthalmologists and a vision therapist. They will walk you through some basics on how to navigate right now. Hang in there," she says.

She turns to Alma.

"I'll have someone come in to schedule him for surgery," she says. Alma thanks her.

When she leaves, we all sit in silence for a minute. Finally, I turn to him.

"Ryder, it's gonna be——"

"Will you go to May's and get Annabelle?" he asks, cutting me off.

"Oh, honey, I'll grab her," Alma says. "That way Mila can stay here with you."

But Ryder shakes his head.

"No, please," he says. "I want her to get to sleep in her own bed tonight. Please."

I swallow and nod, leaning forward to kiss his cheek.

As I go to leave, he reaches for my hand and, by some miracle, actually catches it.

"Take care of her," he says.

28

I wake up before the sun the next morning, that knot in my stomach twisting and turning and burning. Derrick will be bringing Ryder home today, and his surgery has been scheduled for early this coming week.

Alma is coming to pick up Annabelle for a girls' day. We're not quite sure how she will react to Ryder's not being able to see.

I still don't know how I'm supposed to react. Not sure how a four-year-old should.

I MAKE sure everything is spotless—I realize he won't be able to tell, but it's more for his safety. I make sure all the princesses and dolls are picked up from the floor, all the furniture is exactly where it normally is so as not to throw him off.

Finally, I hear Derrick's tires in the gravel outside the house. I meet them at the front door. Derrick hops out and walks around, holding out his arm for Ryder to grab hold of. I almost smile at the sight of them. They are more like brothers than anything else. Loyal to the death.

He leads Ryder up the steps and to the door where I'm waiting. Derrick carries his bags inside while I reach my hands out to him and cup his face.

"I love you," I whisper to him. He closes his eyes and presses his forehead to mine. "We are going to get through this."

He smiles quickly and nods then uses his foot to feel for the doorway. I help him into the living room and ask what he wants for lunch.

"I'm not really hungry," he says. I nod and close the fridge.

"Okay, all your things are back in your room," Derrick says, emerging from the back.

"Thank you, D," I tell him.

"Do you guys need anything else?" he asks. I shake my head, but Ryder calls his name.

"Can you help me out onto the deck?" he asks.

"Oh, I can do that," I interject. Ryder shakes his head.

"No, it's okay. D, do you mind?" he asks. Derrick looks at me then to Ryder.

"Of course," he says, walking toward him and helping him across the room. I watch as he leads Ryder to one of the chairs on the back deck. Ryder says something to him, and I see Derrick's body go straight as a board. He asks Ryder something then he nods. He comes back into the house. He goes back to Derrick's bedroom then back onto the deck. He hands Ryder some sort of envelope then claps him on the back. Ryder reaches a hand up, and Derrick squeezes it.

Derrick makes his way back into the house and grabs his keys off the island.

"He, uh, asked if you could go out there," he says. He looks like he wants to say more, but he presses his lips together and walks out the front door.

Loyal to death.

I take a deep breath and walk out onto the back deck.

It's fairly warm for a winter day in Meade Lake, but I still pull my sweatshirt around me tight. I scoot a chair up next to him and look out at the frozen water.

My first instinct is to comment on the view, not for the cliché of it all, but because it really is breathtaking. I love living here.

But then I remember he can't join in on that, so I switch gears.

"Annabelle was great last night," I say. "She ate all her mac and cheese and went right to bed. I may have let her watch another episode of *Sofia the First* first, but *then* she went to bed."

He smiles as his green eyes stare out at nothing.

He doesn't say anything; he just reaches for the envelope that's on his lap and hands it to me.

"What is this?" I ask. He motions to it, and I take it slowly. I open it and pull out a thick stack of papers. When I flip them over, I feel my heart rate accelerate.

It reads CUSTODY AGREEMENT in thick, black letters.

"Ryder...what is this?"

"I need you to read it," he whispers, closing his eyes and folding his hands in his lap.

I swallow and look down at it.

I can't comprehend a lot of what I'm reading. I'm

not sure if it's the legal jargon or the fact that my name is all over this thing.

My eyes speed from word to word across the pages till I get to the bottom.

Where it has my name listed as the guardian—of Annabelle.

"Ryder, what the hell is this?" I ask, holding it up, hand shaking. He takes in a deep breath and turns to me.

I don't know how, but his eyes find mine, and even though he can't see me, I can still feel him looking right through me.

"What is this?" I ask, my voice shaky and soft.

"I had it written up after that first appointment at Dr. Chandler's," he says, "when I got the diagnosis. In case the cancer wasn't...in case it isn't curable."

I swallow.

"After seeing how she is with you, how she gravitates toward you, how much the two of you love each other...I knew it had to be you. I was going to wait to see how my first scans went post-treatment," he goes on, "but I guess we know."

"Dr. Shidu said they have a plan. After surgery, after treatment...your prognosis is fine. You will be okay. We can't think…" My voice trails off, panic taking over and silencing everything.

"Shh," he says, reaching a hand out. Reluctantly, I reach out to meet his, and he pulls my hand to his lips. He kisses it, squeezing his eyes shut.

"Why are you giving this to me now?" I ask, tears streaming down my face. "You're not dying. You're going to be okay."

A sad smile flickers on his lips.

"I might not die from this," he says, "but I'm not going to be 'okay.'"

I narrow my eyes at him.

"You heard Dr. Shidu," he says. "I might be like this for the rest of my life. Which is why...I need you to take her now."

It feels like a blow to the chest.

"What?" I cry out.

"Just listen to me, please, Mila," he whispers, his voice cracking. "I know this is so much to ask. And you don't owe me any favors... God, with our history, it should be the other way around. I know. But I can't take care of her like this." He motions to his eyes. "I can't help her take a bath, brush her hair, put a damn bandage on her skinned knees. I can't do *anything* like this. And she deserves *everything*. And so do you."

I cover my mouth with my hand to try and stifle the sobs.

"I don't want her, or you, going through life having to be my eyes if this thing sticks. Please, Mila. Take her."

His jaw trembles as he squeezes my hands, pleading with his entire body.

I push my chair back and stand up, yanking my hands from his grasp.

How dare he ask me such an impossible favor? How dare he both give me all I've ever wanted and take it away at the same time?

I walk to the railing and grab it, staring out at the frozen world in front of me. I don't even feel the wind biting at my skin. I just feel the heat of the anger I feel, toward cancer, toward the damn tumor. Toward life in general, for being so unfair. For not giving us enough time.

But then I lift my eyes to him, sitting with his face in his hands. This beautiful mess of a man who has led me to such a wild, uncertain life. And yet, even like this, even unsure how much time we have, I wouldn't trade it for a slow, easy, steady life. I'd keep the pain, the trenches we dug ourselves out of, the complete and utter despair I feel about the idea of possibly losing him. I'd keep it all for the moments where he touches me or brushes my hair back. For the moments he watches me cook or smiles at me while Annabelle and I dance in the living room. I'd keep it all.

I walk to him and wiggle in between his legs. I take his hands from his face and kneel down in front of him. I put them on my face, and then I put my own on his.

"Listen to me," I say. He keeps his eyes closed, but I know I have his attention. "I will never, *ever* leave that little girl. I will always be here for her, no matter what that means. No matter where...no matter where you are. But you are more than your eyes, Ryder Casey."

He lifts his head a bit, his expression pained and unsure about where I'm going.

"All those years ago, when I felt like I was stuck, a sitting duck in a big old lake, you were the one who got me back to shore. Who told me not to be scared. That my parents would make it. That *we* would make it."

"Yeah. Right before I destroyed it all," he says.

"But look where I am now. Six months ago, I had no idea where I was going or what I was doing. I was drowning again. And then I came to you. And I'm back on land. Now, maybe it's your time to let me pull you in."

He leans back in his chair, not buying what I'm saying.

"Ryder, you're her *father*. You are her *everything*. Do you think she wouldn't want you just because you can't *see?*"

He shakes his head and runs a hand over his face.

"How will I—"

"*We.*"

He cocks his head and shoots me a look. For a moment, it feels like he knows exactly where I'm standing.

"It's *we* from now on. Eventually, you will figure things out. Even if...even if your sight never comes back. You will learn how to walk; you will learn how to read; there's therapy and resources and people who are pros at this. Your vision doesn't make you. And it certainly doesn't get to *take* you from us. And neither do you. You don't get to make that decision for us. Got it?"

I lean in closer to his face.

"You're stuck with me," I whisper. "You sure you're ready for that?"

He smiles and leans forward, his hands finding my face again. He pulls my head to his so that our noses touch.

"Born ready," he whispers before kissing me like I've never been kissed in my life.

A kiss that says *nothing is certain, except for how we feel right here in this moment*.

He pulls to his feet and wraps his arms around my back, letting his tongue explore mine. My head drops back, and he kisses my neck, leaving a trail down to my nape. I feel this surge of energy flowing through him, one he hasn't had in a few weeks since the treatment kicked in.

We pull apart for a moment, and he leans into me.

"Lead me inside," he whispers, his voice grizzly and hurried. A spark of excitement flows through me, pooling in my most delicate area.

"Ryder, are you sure?"

"Let's go," he says, reaching his hand out to me. I help him into the living room, and he feels for the furniture. He gets around fairly easily in his own home, and when he gets to the couch, he turns to me and turns a hand up to me. I take it, and he pulls me into him. His hands slide down my body and tug at the hem of my shirt. I take a breath and lift my arms over my head. He pulls the sweater up over it, my undershirt going with it. He unclasps my bra, and chills ripple across my skin.

He leans back onto the couch and holds his arms out. I sink down on top of him, relishing in the way his hands feel on my bare skin. He takes me into his mouth, and I gasp at how well he can love my body. And his hands find every inch of me that needs him. I smile to myself. He doesn't need to see my body; his body remembers every corner of mine, like they were made for each other. It's not that we're pieces that fit together perfectly. It's that we were two uneven, jagged pieces that have ground together, sanding each other until we became a perfect fit.

29

SIX MONTHS LATER

"What about this one?" my mom asks, holding out a little denim dress with a pink bow on the neckline.

I shake my head.

"Not her style," I tell her, rifling through another one of the racks in front of me.

"This one?" she asks me. This one is green with bows on the sleeves. I shake my head again.

"No bows, Ma," I laugh. "She's not really a bow kinda girl."

Mom smiles.

"She might not have your blood in her veins," she says, "but that girl has so much of you in her it's scary."

I look down the aisle of clothes at Annabelle who is happily humming while she slides one piece of clothing after the other around the rack. She's very particular. I love that about her. She's a girl that knows what she likes. I smile as I watch her, perfectly content in her own little world. She has no idea right now that she's mine.

Just as I'm about to walk over to her, I hear my name.

"Mila?" he asks, and I swallow.

I turn slowly toward him. It's been so long since I've seen his face. He looks a little bit older, more wrinkles around his eyes. As he shifts the things in his hands, I notice the twinkle of a wedding band on his finger.

"Luke," I say, breathless. He smiles at me and walks toward me. Without thinking, I pull him in for a hug.

"You look great," he says. Then my mom appears in the aisle, and he pulls her in for a hug, too. He turns back to me. "How are you? I was so sorry to hear about—" He pauses to clear his throat. "I was so sorry to hear about Ryder."

I nod and give the same sad smile I've been giving people for the past eight months or so. I'm really over the pity party that's been thrown for us by every person we know—and even those we don't—over the last year.

Just then, Annabelle stumbles out from the racks of clothes and runs to me.

"I like this one, Mama!" she says, holding up a red jumpsuit. I'm still not quite used to her calling me that, and I still feel a pang of guilt whenever she does. But I'm determined not to let the memory of Maura fade. After all, Annabelle is truly the spitting image of her—at least, what I've gathered from pictures. Absolutely stunning. I keep a picture of Maura framed in our living room, and we talk about her a lot. She *will* know who her mother is. I only hope I'm doing her proud, raising her how Maura would have wanted.

I feel Luke's eyes on me. I turn back to him.

"And who is this?" he asks, his lips turning up into a smile.

"This," I say, pulling Annabelle into me, "is my daughter, Annabelle." I feel my chest puffing as I say it. I love calling her that. He looks at me again, a curious smile on his face. He knows she's not really mine—I was still married to him when she would have been born. But nevertheless, he smiles then kneels down to her.

"Hi, Annabelle," he says.

"Hi. Who are you?" she asks. We both laugh.

"My name is Luke," he says. "I'm an old friend of your...of your mom's. It's so nice to meet you." She smiles and nods, clinging to my hand. He stands back up, and his eyes meet mine.

"It was so good to see you, Mila," he says. I smile and nod. As he turns to walk away, he calls my name again. I turn back.

"I'm so glad he gave you what you wanted most," he says to me. Then, he turns and walks out of the store. I sigh and turn back to the little girl in front of me still holding up the jumpsuit.

I'm a little surprised by the choice; it's...loud. It's bright red with black polka dots all over. On the front is a heart made from gold sequins.

"Wow," I say, "it's so bright and colorful! Are you sure this is the one?" I ask her. You only get your first day of kindergarten outfit once, after all.

She nods enthusiastically.

"I like it because then Daddy can see it, too," she says. My mother and I look at each other then back to her.

"What...what do you mean, baby?" I ask. She walks toward me and pulls the jumpsuit down. She takes my fingers and looks up at me.

"Close your eyes," she tells me. I do. Then, she takes

my fingers in hers and runs them across the sequins, trailing the border of the heart.

"See," she says. "Daddy can see it, too."

I open my eyes, now filled with tears as I stare back at her.

"Yeah, sweet girl," I say, my voice cracking. "And he will love it."

LATER THAT AFTERNOON, I'm looking out the window while she runs across the lawn in her bathing suit. My mom and dad are in the kitchen, grabbing plates and baskets of food and bringing them out to the deck. Derrick is chasing Annabelle across the grass, ducking from the streams of her squirt gun. May and Alma are under the deck, chatting away, and the breeze is making everything feel hazy and perfect in that Meade Lake way.

I look out to the water, and on our dock sits the most perfect man in the world, letting his feet dangle in the water. I smile and slip out the back door. I walk down the dock, letting my shoes scrape across the wood a little bit so he knows I'm coming. I drag my hand across the railings that Derrick installed on either side so that Ryder can come down here on his own.

After the surgery, most of the tumor was gone. Treatment worked on the last of the cancer, and he's officially been in remission for a month and a half.

He can make out some shapes, but he says it's like being in a dark room before your eyes adjust—shadows everywhere.

But we're figuring it out.

We've changed the forms at the shop so that

different ones are printed in different stock so he can tell them apart. He's learning Braille, and we've made some improvements to both the house and the store so it's easier for him to get around. In our house, he barely uses his cane anymore. He knows his way around so well. We got rid of unnecessary furniture and decor that could trip him up.

We're figuring it out. It's hard. But he's still here. And he's still mine.

"Hey, you," he says before I even get all the way to him.

"Hi," I say, sitting down next to him. He slips an arm around my back and pulls me into him for a long kiss.

"How was shopping?" he asks.

"Great. We found a lovely jumpsuit," I tell him. I pause for a moment. "I, uh, ran into Luke."

He tilts his head and turns to me.

"Oh?"

"Yeah. He said he was sorry about what happened to you. And, uh, that he was glad you gave me what I always wanted."

He smiles curiously.

"Meaning what?"

"Meaning, after all this time, you're not the one who took everything away. You're the one who gave me everything."

He pulls me in for another kiss, and I snuggle back against him as we stare out over the water.

"Mostly orange, with some streaks of magenta," I whisper just as I do every night so that we can share the sunset together. "It's the prettiest thing I've ever seen."

"Can't be. I'm looking at her right now," he says. I kiss his cheek.

The waves from the wakes of boats flying by lap up against our feet and the dock. I breathe in the moment, soaking in the peace of having all I could ever need. I look back at him, still with the same boyish charm he's had since I was sixteen.

He's a rope, and he might have some fray to him. There might be some knots along the way, but if I follow him, if I hang on, I know I'll get back to shore.

THE MEADE LAKE SERIES

Did you enjoy Back to Shore?

Order the next three books in the Meade Lake series now!

    Stones Unturned
    In Winters Past

ACKNOWLEDGMENTS

I have been sitting on pieces of this series for over ten years now, and I am so excited for the world to meet the Meade Lake crew. I want to thank my fellow indie friends who are constantly letting me bounce ideas off of them, giving me advice, letting me vent, and cheering me on. I love the tribe we have, and I am so thankful for you ladies!

I want to thank my Gram and Pop for giving us the place where I made so many memories, and the place where this series was born from—the lake house. Some of the best times of my life were made there, and without all those lake trips and mountain air, this series would never have seen the light of day.

I want to thank my family for constantly being in my corner with all this writing stuff. Even when I don't believe in myself, you do it for me. I can never repay you for fighting alongside me for my dreams.

Cass and Pay, I wouldn't be here with the two of you constantly having my back in this! I love you!

Will, B, and LG, I hope you know how much I love you and how grateful I am every day that I have the three of you.

ABOUT TAYLOR

T.D. Colbert is a romance and women's fiction author. When she's not chasing her kids or hanging with her husband, she's probably under her favorite blanket, either reading a book or writing one. She lives in Maryland, where she was born and raised. For more information, visit www.tdcolbert.com.

Follow T.D. on Instagram and Twitter, @taydanaewrites, and on Facebook, Author T.D. Colbert, for information on upcoming books!

Are you a blogger or a reader who wants in on some secret stuff? Sign up for my newsletter, and join **TDC's VIPs** - T.D.'s reader group on Facebook for exclusive information on her next books, early cover reveals, give-aways, and more!

OTHER BOOKS BY T.D. COLBERT:

T.D. Colbert's Author Page

NOTE FROM THE AUTHOR

Dear Reader,

I can't tell you what it means that you've decided, out of all of the books in all the world, to read mine.

If you enjoyed reading it as much as I enjoyed writing it, please consider leaving an Amazon or GoodReads review (or both!). Reviews are crucial to a book's success, and I can't thank you enough for leaving one (or a few!)!

Thank you for taking the time to read *Back to Shore*.

Always,
   TDC
   www.tdcolbert.com
   @taydanaewrites

Made in United States
Orlando, FL
28 January 2023

29158628R00150